"Cinderella is every little girl's first romance novel, at least where the heroine is awake for most of the story."

~ Kat Young

one

...Kat Young, her tousled auburn mane falling to bare shoulders, hung from a yardarm by tightly-bound wrists, her lush bosom swelling from the top of her once-elegant, but now ragged corseted dress. A starboard broadside tipped the three-hundred-ton man-o'-war, Queen Anne's Revenge, hard to port and for a moment she dangled dangerously close to the fins of the tiger sharks circling in hungry anticipation of the bloody detritus of battle. Then the ship swung back to starboard and she struggled against her bonds as musket balls, fired from the approaching frigate flying the Union Jack, whizzed around her.

Above her on the bridge paced the pirate leader Captain Jack, with cruelly-handsome chiseled features, his jet-black curly hair accented by a touch of grey at his temples. Resplendent in black velvet coat and breaches, lace ruffles at his neck and wrists, and with twin black bone-handled pistols in hand, he shouted to the gun crews, "Reload, you scurvy dogs, or it'll be your heads on the pikes in Port Royal!"

Undaunted by the fusillade from the Queen Ann's roaring guns, the frigate bore down on them, its bow cannon flinging iron missiles through the pirate vessel's sails, one of which sheared off the mid-mast, nearly missing Captain Jack's lovely captive as it crashed to the deck, crushing an unlucky pirate.

"Fire, fire, you sons of whores!" roared the pirate captain, too late, as the British ship pulled alongside. Grappling hooks were flung, a party of British marines swarmed aboard, and combat raged, hand to hand.

Captain Jack emptied his pistols into the backs of two British soldiers, then sensing the tide was turning, slid down the railing to his desperate prisoner, the only place on deck not yet overrun by marines. Drawing his cutlass, he hacked at the rope above her until she fell into his arms. "Curse you, monster!" she screamed as he flung her over his shoulder, her hands still tightly bound.

Captain Jack turned to the aft deck, but his way was blocked by an intruder, who quickly found himself impaled on the dark captain's sword. Mounting a stairway, he fought his way through the melee, slashing

3

at the invaders and shoving his men aside, until he reached the lifeboat hanging from the poop deck, into which he unceremoniously dumped his struggling captive. Then he leapt in after her and cut the rope, sending the tiny craft hurtling to the sea.

Kat screamed in frustration as Captain Jack laid into the oars, pulling away from the battle raging on his ship. After weeks of imprisonment in the captain's cabin, weeks of being ravished by this evil man and his first mate whenever the mood struck them, sometimes in tandem, it was too much to bear that rescue was so near, yet still out of reach. She looked back to the battle scene, then to the beach their small craft was making for. Following her desperate gaze, Captain Jack laughed derisively and sneered, "Kat? Your car's ready"...

She looked at him, uncomprehending. What nonsense was this? What fresh insult?

"Kat?" the body shop service manager repeated.

"Oh right, sorry," she said, the sounds of battle and the smell of the salt air fading in the remote sea lanes of her mind.

"Wow, you were really in the zone," Jack smiled.

"Thinking about, you know, work," She murmured as she closed her computer.

"I know the name of that tune," he smiled. "Takes me, like, an hour to unwind when I get home."

Jack had to be the best looking service manager in LA, model handsome, with chiseled features and just a touch of grey at the temples in otherwise jet black curly hair. And, of course, a fat gold wedding ring.

"Sorry for the delay, the shop foreman wanted to do a quick respray and polish on the door. Anyway, the frame straightened out fine. I test drove her and she tracks perfectly. Nobody would ever know she's been hit."

"Unless they check the Internet," said Kat, smiling at the thought of her MINI being a girl.

"Yeah, that's true now," he said, "nobody has any secrets anymore." He handed her the paperwork. "Cashier has your keys. Be careful out there, we don't want to see you back here for a while."

"You and my insurance company," she said. "If it happens again I'll be riding the bus."

§

Kat put the paperwork on the counter. The cashier was on her phone, the call apparently important enough to not notice her. Kat couldn't decide which she found more disturbing, the amount of thigh beneath the hem of the girl's ridiculously short skirt, the length of her heavily-lacquered nails, embossed with tiny scorpions, or the size of her breasts, which were either surgically enhanced or revealed a genetic mutation that would fascinate anthropologists, at least male anthropologists.

"Excuse me?" Kat ventured cautiously.

Nothing.

Kat said "Hello?" a little more assertively. This had some effect, the girl lifted a finger in the air to indicate it would only be a minute. Kat looked out the window at her car. The red MINI convertible did, indeed, look good as new. It was even washed, something she couldn't remember seeing in at least six months. To wash one's car, one had to actually leave one's place of work. She looked at the courtesy TV monitor on the wall. A group of women, sitting six abreast on a low stage, were screaming at each other as the audience screamed at them. Marty, Kat's boyfriend, would have muted the sound with his secret pocket universal remote as soon as he sat down. Someday she was going to read that he'd been beaten to death by an angry geriatric mob in a doctor's waiting room. She turned back to the cashier. "I'm sorry, I've been here for, like, two hours, and I was already late."

The girl said, "Call you later," getting to her feet abruptly and snapping the phone shut to signal her unhappiness at the interruption. She picked up Kat's paperwork. "It looks like your deductible is $600. Check or plastic?"

"Definitely plastic," said Kat bringing out her wallet. She handed over her credit card. Aware the cashier had looked critically at <u>her</u> nails, Kat put her hands to her sides self-consciously as the girl swiped her card, adding "manicure" to the list of thing one must leave work to accomplish. The cashier handed her the credit slip and a pen. "So, I guess you're a Scorpio," said Kat as she scrawled her name on the voucher.

"Pisces," replied the cashier, giving it an "as if" inflection as she stapled the paperwork with scorpion-tipped fingers.

§

Kat drove her car out of the body shop's parking lot, merging smoothly with the late-morning West Los Angeles traffic. As she approached the red light at the end of the block she noticed the hub of the steering wheel wasn't perfectly flat while the car was driving straight. Marty would torture her about this. She briefly considered turning around and driving back to the shop, but couldn't bear the thought of another minute in those ragged vinyl chairs. She stopped at the light next to a shiny new Porsche, still wearing the cardboard dealer sign in the license plate frame. The driver had stylishly tousled blond hair and an Ashton Kutcher chin. He looked over and smiled at her. *Nice eyes.* She looked at him again and he was still smiling at her. *Really nice eyes.* She smiled hastily, then looked back at the intersection. *Ashton. Definitely an "Ashton."*

The light turned green, and she was a little surprised to see the new Porsche driver didn't match her acceleration. *What did you expect? Silly, anyway, thinking about people in cars at stoplights.* Still, she felt that familiar desperation wash over her, that feeling she wasn't in control of her life. She gripped the bottom of the steering wheel with both hands, pressing her wrists together. *Would it be so bad to be a pirate's captive?*

. . . Kat noticed Captained Black looking back at his ship with concern, and for the first time saw worry in his unfailingly stern visage. With the last ounce of strength in her body, she stretched to see above the gunwale, and what she saw sparked a ray of hope in her breast: Lieutenant-Commander Ashton Moorcroft, resplendent in his white, blue and gold uniform, pressed against the rail of the poop deck holding off a gaggle of pirates with only his saber and raw courage.

Kat screamed "Ashton!" but instantly regretted it when he turned at her voice, and in that moment of lowered guard a pirate painted a strip of crimson on his forearm with his cutlass. Turning back to the fray, Ashton ran the blackguard through, then quickly dispatched the other three. Turning his attention back to the departing lifeboat, he jammed his sword into its scabbard and climbed the railing. Balancing there, he removed his lieutenant-commander's hat, revealing extravagantly tousled blond hair. Without hesitation, he tossed his hat into the sea and followed it in a perfect arcing dive.

"The sharks'll have him, and good riddance," sneered Captain Jack, leaning into the oars. And, indeed, a white fin veered off from the circling troop and headed straight toward the Lieutenant-Commander. But Ashton kicked off his boots and launched into an Olympian crawl, managing to stay just ahead of the huge hungry fish.

"Impossible!" muttered Captain Jack, who dropped the oars and set to work reloading his pistols.

"Coward," sneered Kat. "You fear to face him man to man."

"Either way, he'll be just as dead," said Captain Jack. "Anyway, look at the distance. He'll soon be exhausted and drowned like a rat."

Kat strained to chart her rescuer's progress, more concerned now for his safety than her own. "Ashton, go back!" she cried.

But Ashton redoubled his effort, actually pulling away from the shark, which had now been joined by two others. Seeing this, Captain Jack pulled harder on the oars, cursing the bloody fool for his rashness, until the bloody fool was within a stone's throw of the boat, at which point the pirate captain stood in the rocking boat and drew his pistols from his belt. With one last

Herculean stroke, Ashton reached the boat, throwing an arm over the side, and looked up into the angry face of Kat's tormentor.

"So I'll have the pleasure of dispatching you myself, you fool," Captain Jack scowled as he cocked his pistols. But in that instant Kat threw herself forward, rolling behind him and planted both feet in the velvety seat of his breeches, sending him tumbling over Ashton in the sea and, not incidentally, causing the pistols to discharge harmlessly into the water.

Ashton turned to his adversary just in time, as the pirate shot to the surface with dagger drawn and set upon him, and the sworn enemies spun in a life-or-death struggle in the dark sea.

Hooking her bonds on the oarlock, Kat pulled herself up and watched anxiously as, in turn, each man had the upper hand. Then, to her horror, they disappeared beneath the waves.

"Ashton!" cried Kat, desperate for some sign he lived.

The seconds ticked by as she scanned the now placid water, interrupted only by the arrival of the sharks.

"Oh, please live, my love," she cried, desperately.

Then, to her horror, the ocean boiled with blood as the sharks attacked beneath the waves.

"My God! Ashton! You can't be gone!" she wailed.

"Well, the report of my demise may have been somewhat exaggerated."

Kat spun around to see him clinging to the opposite side of the boat. Then the unlucky man below was the black-hearted pirate after all. "Thank God," cried Kat as she fell on her lover, helping him into the boat. Ashton swayed, weak from blood loss from his wound.

"Oh, my God, you're wounded," said Kat.

"It's nothing to the wound my heart would have suffered if I'd lost you, Kat," said Ashton. He drew his sword and cut her bonds, and she fell into his arms and into his kiss, the deepest, hottest kiss two lovers ever shared in the history of the world... which exploded in her face amid a flurry of talcum powder and a metallic crashing sound, then deflated, as the MINI spun violently counter-clockwise, the result of having hit the left rear fender of an otherwise perfect bright red 1949 GMC pickup truck.

All was quiet for a moment. Then something fell off the front of Kat's car, clattering on the pavement. She muttered, "Shit."

There was no movement from the truck. Apparently the person was as shocked as she was. She took off her sun glasses, which had been smashed by the airbag, threw open her door and flew out of the car, screaming at the truck's open window, "Hello...red light? Are you friggin' blind?"

11

The truck's door pushed open and a good looking enough guy to have normally made Kat feel a little shy stepped down to the tarmac, his straight, shoulder-length hair just touching the collar of his pink oxford shirt, tail-out over slightly ragged jeans and black Converse All-Stars.

"Look at my car!" screamed Kat. "I just had it fixed!"

The damaged pickup owner regarded this mad woman, her face and shoulders covered in airbag talc, with the exception of the area around her eyes, which had been shielded by her sunglasses, making her look vaguely raccoon-like. He resisted the urge to laugh or even smile and turned his attention to his fender, which was pushed against the wheel of his truck.

"Please tell me you have insurance. Hello? Are you even listening to me?" said Kat, anguish beginning to creep into her voice.

"Hey guy, I was right behind her. She ran the light," someone nearby commented.

Kat looked around. It was Ashton, or, rather, the driver of the new Porsche. He stuck his arm out the window of his car, a business card in his fingers.

"Here's my card, if you need a witness or anything."

Kat's victim walked over, took it and thanked him, then walked back to his truck as the Porsche drove off. He knelt by the fender and pulled it free of the wheel.

"I'm sorry, I thought it was green," mumbled Kat. She turned to her car to get her purse. "Look, I have insurance, not for long after this, but..." She spun around when she heard the truck's door slam and the engine turn over. "What are you doing?" she called out as the driver put the truck in gear and drove off. "Wait! I said I was sorry."

two

A Venti Starbuck's at hand, Kat tore into the memo like the mortal enemy it was, to be dispatched with ruthless fury. The last thing she needed after dealing with the tow truck taking her car back to the body shop thirty minutes after she'd picked it up (the unbelieving look on Jack's face!) was shit from her boss, but this work was supposed to have been done for the meeting she'd missed. Her phone vibrated in her purse. She took it out and the caller ID read: "Jean Young," her mother once again demonstrating her uncanny knack for bad timing. She thought about it, then pressed the green button.

"Hi, Mom."

"Kat? It's your mother."

Kat shook her head in wonder. Not only did nearly every phone in existence display the name of the caller, but by now she found her mother's voice quite recognizable, and she'd just said, "Hi, Mom."

"What's up?" said Kat, putting her on speaker so she could keep typing.

"We haven't spoken in a while and I wanted to be sure you don't forget your birthday."

"Like I could if I wanted to."

"Do you want to come over for dinner that night? I could pick up a cake at Ralph's."

Kat's mother famously didn't cook, beyond heating things up on the stove or in the microwave. Kat remembered her explaining, after drinking half a box of white wine, that it had something to do with women's liberation.

"You can bring a friend," Jean hastened to add, causing a twinge of guilt that her mother might have figured out she was uncomfortable dealing with her alone.

"Thanks, but Tina and Juanita have something planned at a nightclub or something."

"But this is a special birthday," sniffed Jean.

"That's why we're going to a nightclub, Mom."

Tina Prem, the petite Asian-American hottie with whom she shared a cubicle wall, stuck her head in. As usual, Tina looked like a miniature model, dressed in a ruffled pink blouse, Capri pants and four-inch-high black Mary Janes, her face framed by choppy cuts of burgundy-highlighted hair. Tina lived in an alternate universe when it came to corporate dress codes.

"I have to go, Mom, one of my colleagues needs me."

"We didn't get to talk about what you want for your birthday," said Jean.

"Mom, it's just another day."

"You're going to be thirty. That's a milestone."

"More like a millstone," said Kat. "I have to go; I'll call you later."

"OK, goodbye dear."

"Bye, Mom."

Sighing, Kat pushed the red button and turned to Tina. "My mother."

"I figured that when you called her Mom," said Tina. "So, we missed you at Stuckie's Monday morning torture session." Her eyes narrowed."Is that air-bag powder?"

"Is it still there?" said Kat, brushing off her shoulders.

"Is it still there? You look like a mime."

"Oh, baby doll, don't tell me you had another accident in your cute little car." It was Juanita, a stack of contracts clutched to the synthetic blouse tucked into the too-tight brown polyester pants she'd poured her short, stocky figure into that morning.

"I had another accident in my cute little car."

"Anybody hurt?" clucked Juanita as she tucked the contracts under her arm, pulled a tissue from the box on the desk and wiped the remaining talc smudges from Kat's face.

"Only my pride, insurability, rapidly dwindling bank account and, of course, my car."

Juanita started to put the tissue in her mouth.

"Please don't spit on that," said Kat.

"Sorry," said Juanita, "force of habit."

Kat turned back to her work. "The truck I hit, on the other hand, has a slightly bent fender. I think I scared the guy more than the accident. He didn't even wait to get my contact info, practically laid rubber getting out of there. He was kinda' cute, too, in a Bridges of Madison County kind of way," said Kat, unaware that Rebecca Stuckie was standing outside the entry to her cubicle, behind her friends.

"Are you copying those?" Rebecca said curtly, indicating the contracts under Juanita's arm.

Juanita said, "Just about to," and ducked past her.

Rebecca fixed Tina with THE LOOK.

"I'll be getting back to my hamster wheel," said Tina as she scurried away.

Then Rebecca turned her gimlet eye on Kat. "You missed the meeting. Not a very good example for your team."

"I had a car accident," said Kat. Ms. Stuckey, unlike her conservative suit, was no longer a size eight, a fact that caused Kat to rivet her attention on Rebecca's eyes whenever she spoke to her. Rebecca had been impressed that Kat seemed to be so attentive on their first meeting. Now it made her vaguely uncomfortable.

"Wasn't that, like, three weeks ago? You said they gave you a rental car," said Rebecca.

"I had another accident this morning," sighed Kat.

Before Rebecca could fully process this she was interrupted by a disarmingly resonate, "Good morning, Rebecca," and she turned to greet Jason Stevens with an urgent smile. It never ceased to amaze Kat that a woman of Rebecca's intelligence and position could be reduced to jelly in the presence of someone like Jason, as if she'd never seen a weirdly handsome, inexplicably single senior VP in a grey Armani suit before. *Disgusting*, she thought, straightening up and pushing her shoulders back.

"Do you need me for something?" purred Rebecca, her chest subtly inflating (as if it needed any more inflation).

"Actually, I'm after Kat," smiled Jason.

"Well, right, then," said Rebecca, when it was clear no further explanation was forthcoming. She turned back to Kat. "Please remember, Kat, Monday Meeting isn't optional." She gave Jason an awkward parting smile, then lurched off in the direction of her office.

Kat smiled up at Jason, trying to decide if she'd heard him correctly. *"I'm after Kat."* Of course, *he only meant he needs to speak with me.* "What can I do you for?" *Shit, idiotic thing to say.*

Jason entered her tiny space and sat on the edge of her desk close enough that she got a faint hit of his scent. It didn't smell like cologne, more like soap. *Clean.*

"I just wanted to thank you. Impressive work on the MartCo/Kelly merger proposal," he said.

"No problem," said Kat, "except for getting yelled at by my boss." *I wonder if I'm still wearing airbag talc?*

"Why? You did an amazing job," he said.

"She wants all projects submitted through her. She gets very weird about it."

"You mean territorial," he said. "I'll deal with it. In the meantime, the merger proposal is a go, and we're going to be pulling out all the stops. I'd like you on board."

Kat suddenly saw a light at the end of the Stuckey tunnel. *Be cool. He'll respect you more if he sees you're a team player.* "Great," said Kat, "assuming you get Rebecca's approval."

"Absolutely," said Jason. "Do you have a minute to help with the agenda?"

Kat hesitated. "Now?"

"If you're not, you know, saving lives or anything."

He's looking at my forehead. Is that stupid powder still... "I just need to finish this email," she said, indicating the message on her screen that should have been sent two hours ago.

"No problem," smiled Jason. "I have a meeting at one, but I'm open until then."

He was barely gone before Tina appeared, her bag over her shoulder. Kat already had her compact out, checking her face.

"I'm after Kat," Tina said, mimicking Jason's man-voice.

"We have zero privacy here," said Kat, spitting on a napkin and wiping the last of the powdery residue from her ears. "Anyway, he's nice."

"Nice? More like hot," said Tina.

"I have a boyfriend."

"You have Marty," said Tina.

"We're actually having dinner tonight," said Kat.

"A week-night dinner date?" wondered Tina. "What's the occasion?"

"I don't know, he said he had something important he wants to talk to me about."

Tina was suddenly very interested. "You don't think…"

Kat laughed. "Not a chance. But he did bring up living together a few months ago."

Kat noticed Tina had her purse under her arm. "Where are you going?"

"Uh, lunch? What the rest of the world does when they're hungry? Want to come?"

"Can't. I was already behind before this morning's debacle."

"Can I bring you something?"

"I'll just get a bag of chips from the machine."

"Don't forget to get a bag for Jason," Tina said.

"What do you mean?" said Kat, but Tina was already gone. *No privacy at all*, thought Kat. *I need an office with a ceiling and a door. And a thirty-six-hour day.*

20

She looked at the unfinished email, and sighed. *I'm after Kat.*

…Working in the circle of a single light over her desk, Senior Vice President Kat Young finished running the numbers, again, and two and two still equaled three. She tousled her thick auburn hair in frustration, then spun her chair around and looked out on the nighttime city through the floor-to-ceiling window of her twentieth floor office aerie, thoughtfully tenting her fingers to her lips. It didn't make sense. It had been a banner year for the company, but they were still losing money hand over fist. And how did the trade journals know in advance of the stockholders meeting? It was almost as if someone inside the company, someone very high up inside the company, were engaging in sabotage.

She turned back to her desk, and her eyes fell on the drawer holding the flash drive with the security program she'd cajoled out of Max, the IT guy with the hopeless crush on her. Kat saw nothing wrong with using her female powers when it suited her, especially for good. She slid the drawer open and inserted the drive into her computer, entering from memory the sixteen letter and number password Max had finally grudgingly given her. Clicking on "search," she settled back in her chair as the program scanned every email sent by a Globus Company employee in the last year.

Watching the blur of data fly by on the screen she barely noticed the light knock at her partially opened door, and looked up to see Senior Vice President Jason Stevens, holding two cardboard cups of steaming coffee. "I had a feeling you'd still be here," he said.

He walked over to her desk and Kat briefly considered shutting the program down. What she was doing was completely against company policy, and quite possibly illegal as well, but for some reason she trusted that he would get that desperate times called for desperate measures. He put the coffees on her desk.

"Sorry, it's just from the machine," he said. "Half and half, one Splenda."

"I can't believe you remembered that from just having coffee with me once," said Kat, removing the plastic cover on the coffee. She briefly savored the aroma before taking a sip, a nod to her precept to always stop and smell the coffee.

"Is that what I think it is?" said Jason, looking at her screen.

"Maybe," said Kat cryptically. "But I've gone over and over it, and the only thing I can think of is that this is all coming from someone inside."

"I'm beginning to think the same thing. Don't worry, this will just be between us. Desperate times call for desperate measures."

Kat smiled at this, thinking how often and perfectly their minds mirrored each other.

He sat on the corner of her desk, looking at the screen intently, and she sensed once again that faint, subtle intoxicating scent, not of cologne—he didn't wear cologne—but of clean, of a fine wool suit stored in a cedar-lined closet and the verbena soap he'd showered with.

The program locked, indicating it had a positive or positives.

"Does that mean what I think it means?" said Jason.

"It does," said Kat as she opened the file, which held dozens of emails. They read the header information at the same moment. "Rebecca Stuckie," they said simultaneously.

"She has the CEO's ear and total trust," said Jason. "This complicates matters terribly."

"Well, obviously," said Kat.

Jason turned to her, and she looked up into his eyes. "That's not what I mean," he said gently. "There is something I urgently need to discuss with you."...

"What is it, Jason?" Kat asked, that familiar unsettled feeling in her stomach.

"I need these consolidated and labeled before you leave today," he said, his voice oddly harsh and feminine...

"What?" said Kat, looking at Rebecca as if she were an insane stranger who had spoken to her randomly from an angry crowd.

"I said I need these consolidated and labeled before you leave today," repeated Rebecca. "And where's Tina?"

"She went to lunch late," said Kat.

"Well, tell her I want to see her as soon as she's back," said Rebecca, scowling at her watch as she walked out.

Kat considered the new stack of folders on her desk. *My God.* She looked back at the unfinished email on her screen, the words echoing in her brain like a Barbara Cartland title, "*I'm after Kat.*" Decisively, she got out her compact, touched up her mascara and lipstick, picked up her iPad and strode directly to Senior Vice President Jason Steven's office, with only a quick stop to check in the women's room mirror for airbag talc and to tousle her hair.

The door to Jason's office was ajar. Hearing his voice as he spoke on the phone, she knocked lightly, then pushed it open.

Jason was in the chair behind his huge walnut desk, his back to the door, facing the floor-to-ceiling window of his twentieth floor office aerie. "We think it could be huge," he said as he spun his chair around and indicated for Kat to take a seat on the sofa at the far end of the room, adding, "One of my team members just walked in." He held up his finger to let Kat know he was almost done, then turned back to the window. "Uh huh…right…yes…absolutely…we're on it."

Kat loved the thought that she was on his "team," although she was still worried about Rebecca. She decided she'd already said enough about it for today, but would definitely bring it up later as her professional relationship with Jason deepened.

"Right, I'll keep you posted," said Jason, finishing up, then dropped the phone in its cradle and turned his chair back to face her.

"That was the big guy," said Jason.

"Mr. Martin?" said Kat, surprised.

Jason walked over to her and sat on the arm of the sofa. "He agrees this could be <u>the</u> turnaround operation for the company. And he referenced your report."

Backlit by the warm afternoon light from the window, Jason looked otherworldly, like an angel in a $2,000 suit. This, and the faint scent she noticed again (cedar? verbena?) made her slightly light-headed.

…"I've felt for some time this was an area we should be in," said Kat firmly, aware an extra button was open on her blouse, revealing a hint of her swelling bosom, "an unrealized opportunity for the company. I'm surprised Rebecca even let you see my report. Innovation is a very low priority in her department."

"That's something I need to discuss with you. We suspect she may be involved in some activity that isn't in the best interests of the company. We may need for you *to quietly gather some information for us. It may involve some risk."*

"I'm prepared to do whatever is necessary," said Kat, "you know you can count on me."

"I do," said Jason earnestly, "which is why the situation is so complicated."

"What do you mean, Jason?" said Kat, afraid of the answer.

He just looked at her for a moment. "God, you have beautiful eyes, I could lose myself in them," he said, and removed her glasses gently, the way the ophthalmologist does with both hands.

"Jason, are you sure about this?" worried Kat.

He leaned in slightly towards her, his lips promising the deepest, hottest kiss two lovers ever shared in the history of the world and said, "We'll want Starkovitch, Bradley and Cohen on board. Can you set up something for the fifteenth? Uh, Kat?"…

Kat started. Jason was standing now, looking at her with concern.

"Are you OK?"

"Yeah, I'm…I'm fine."

She took her glasses off and pinched the bridge of her nose, then took a deep breath. "I had kind of a car accident today?"

"Wow, hey, I'm sorry," said Jason, "were you hurt?"

"Just punched in the face with the airbag, but I think I am getting a headache."

"Hey, we can pick this up later. I can't believe you're even here."

"God, I have so much work to do, but I think I might go home early." She stood up, but hesitated, a little awkward. "I'll review my notes, in case there was anything I didn't include in the report that might be useful."

"That will be great," said Jason. "I'm really looking forward to working with you on this."

"It was awesome to hear you say team member. There hasn't been a lot of 'team' in my department," said Kat.

"I think we know the problem there," Jason said as he walked back to his desk, making Kat feel vaguely traitorous.

Kat said as she went to the door. "Well, OK then. I should have time to work on it this week."

"Great," Jason repeated absently, already focused on his dayplanner.

§

Kat stepped off the elevator into the granite lobby and walked towards the huge glass doors at the entrance to the building, the laptop bag hanging from her shoulder even heavier than usual because of the work Rebecca had piled on and the work she'd promised Jason. It felt weird to be leaving at four, and she was feeling seriously disoriented, so much so she regretted getting the rental car. All she needed was to have another accident the day of the accident she had picking up a car which had just been repaired from an accident.

"See you tomorrow, Gus," she said to the security guard at his desk by the entrance, who nodded "Have a nice night, Kat," without looking up from the bank of video monitors.

"Thank you, I have other plans," said Kat.

§

Kat found the beige rental Taurus in the lot. *All I'm doing is driving,* she thought, inserting the key. *All my mental resources are focused on driving. I am a bionic driving machine.*

She pulled into the heavy Los Angeles traffic, every other vehicle a potential enemy, and replayed the conversation with Jason. *Awesome.* She shook her head. *I actually said awesome! I hate the word. And bad-mouthing Rebecca. Jesus, Kat.* She stopped for a light. *Marty on a weeknight. How is he even a real boyfriend when those words don't go together? Then there's the "standing date," meaning he doesn't have to do anything but show up. What am I doing in this relationship? He's not even a vegetarian, well, fishatarian. Is fishatarian a word?* The light turned green. She realized she felt safer in the bigger car. *Well, yeah, after two smash-ups in a month.* It wasn't cute, though. The MINI's cute. *Not at the moment.*

Kat drove the Taurus into the garage under her building and parked in her space, which was tight even for the MINI, thanks to the SUV's parked on either side. She squeezed out with her laptop and purse, and briefly considered taking the stairs. It would be her only exercise of the day, but there had been a pungent wet spot on the bottom level when she'd come down to the garage that morning. She pressed the elevator button. *I've got to find a place with gated parking,* she thought as the elevator hummed to life. *It isn't just the pee, what about some psycho rapist waiting in the back of my car?* The doors opened and she stepped in. *Another reason to have the MINI—only room for a child-sized psycho rapist in the back seat.* There was another wet spot reeking of stale piss in the corner of the elevator, and evidently this thoughtful person had asparagus for lunch. Kat whispered, "Mother of God," as the doors closed. *Too late to hold my breath, I'd just be holding in pee vapor.* The elevator lumbered up, the numbers laboriously climbing to "3." As she stepped off, she remembered she hadn't checked her mail in the lobby...

§

Kat let herself into her open floor-plan one-bedroom apartment and slapped the mail on the counter above the sink. She'd taken the stairs on the return trip to the lobby and the pee in the stairwell had ripened in the course of the day. *Got to get a place with a gated garage.* She looked at the boxes of books stacked in the corner as she dropped her purse and laptop on the table. *And room for some bookshelves.* Or she could sell the books on eBay. That's what she should do. Clean house. But she knew as soon as she did she'd want to reread one of them. She kind of felt like doing it now. It was a little past five. Marty wasn't supposed to pick her up until seven-thirty, assuming he was on time, which was a stupid assumption. She should use the time to work on Rebecca's reports, but instead she opened one of the boxes. There it was, right on top, *A Pirate's Passion*, by Smilla Rhodes, who would never know she'd almost killed one of her most loyal readers that day.

She put the book on the counter next to the mail (bills) and opened the fridge. A bit of digging revealed a half-empty bottle of white wine. She pulled the cork and sniffed it, then poured herself a glass, looking at the cover of the book, strong arms enfolding heaving bosom, the jaw line, the flowing blond hair, a little over one eye. *That asshole in the Porsche was nothing like an Ashton.* Sipping the wine, she opened the paperback to a random chapter, and immediately fell under its spell. The familiar narrative, the desperate reckless lovers.

Kat paused and looked around the room. It had been six months since Marty had suggested they get a place together, not "a few," as she'd suggested to Tina. But of course she'd have to take the initiative, like everything else they did. Maybe Marty was all she should expect. She laughed to herself. *Maybe Marty*. He hated that.

She sat in her favorite chair. It was cream leather and oversized, an extravagance. She kicked off her shoes and tucked her feet under her. *What kind of guy absently mentions living together once, then it doesn't come up again for six months? Marty*. She drank some more wine, letting it warm her empty stomach, then returned to the story. She'd read it at least three times. Smilla Rhodes captured that longing so perfectly.

§

Kat's phone rang at precisely seven-forty-five. She knew it was Marty without looking; he hadn't come to her door while picking her up since their first date. She'd ended up nearly finishing the book and hadn't changed her clothes or done anything to her face, but felt only a twinge of panic about that, thanks to two more glasses of wine. She answered it.

It was Marty. "Hey, I'm down here. Sorry I'm late," he said.

Kat said, "I'll be right down," slipping on her shoes. She went to the bathroom and looked in the mirror. She peed. She looked in the mirror again and briefly considered putting on fresh lipstick, then decided whatever.

Remembering the panic ride in the elevator, Kat took the stairs. They were equally disgusting, but at least she wouldn't be trapped with the pee, waiting for the fire department to free her in the event of a power failure. She held her breath for the three flights, exhaling hard as she exited the stairwell into the lobby. Pushing open one of the glass doors, she saw Marty's BMW 3-Series (four doors, of course) at the curb. *Standing date*, she thought, stepping down the concrete stairs to the walk, her purse over her shoulder. It <u>sounded</u> uncomfortable.

She reached his car, but didn't bother to try the door. Marty would never sit in an unlocked car because someone might sneak up and kill him, which Kat was considering at the moment, because he was looking at his iPhone while she was standing there like an idiot. She rapped on the glass and he remote-unlocked the door.

"Hey, thanks," Kat said, sliding onto the seat and closing the door.

"No problem," he said absently, still focused on his fucking phone. Marty was a near-total irony-free zone.

"So, where do you want to go?"

Kat, looking at him in disgust, didn't answer. Finally he looked up. "What?" he said, then got it and put his phone on the console. "Sorry, Sabrina tweets now about everything she does. Why does she think anyone would be interested that she's at the gym and whoever used the elliptical trainer didn't wipe the sweat off when they were done?"

"Good question," said Kat as she fastened her seatbelt, "since you can't seem to get enough of it."

"You're the one who said I should act like I'm interested in what my daughter's doing," he said as he put the car into gear, checked his mirror and pulled away from the curb.

"I believe it was 'take an interest,' not *act* interested," said Kat.

"Whatever. Where do you want to go?"

"Today I got shit from my boss, three times, dealt with the psycho IT guy twice because our company software drives PC's crazy and had a car accident. You decide."

"You can't be serious. You had another accident?" he said, emphasizing "another" in a really irritating manner.

"Yeah, but I wasn't seriously injured, thanks for asking. Look, I seriously need a glass of wine. Could you please just drive us somewhere?"

"You have no idea where you want to go?" he said, a vague whine creeping into his tone.

"Yes: someplace you choose."

"What if you don't like it?" Marty was starting to crack from the pressure.

"Then I'll despise you till my dying breath."

§

Kat, her menu folded on the table next to a red napkin and paper-wrapped chopsticks, tried to make out the pattern in the red-velvet-flocked wallpaper, avoiding the stupid flatscreen TV hanging from the ceiling above the bar.

"So how bad was it?" Marty said, not looking up from his menu.

"What?" said Kat, dragging herself back from the velvet Rorschach.

"The crash. Is your car OK?"

"No, it's not," she said.

"So, you have another rental," he said, turning the page.

"Yeah, but I'm thinking of just taking the bus for a while."

Marty finally looked up, aghast. "You can't take the bus in LA. Only, you know, maids and nannies take the bus."

"Nice," sighed Kat.

"You know what I mean," Marty said, as the waitress arrived with Kat's white wine and his Amstel Light.

"Ready to order?" asked the waitress, whipping out her pad and pen.

"You sure there isn't something you'd like?" Marty said, desperately.

"Choose. Make a decision," said Kat.

Marty stared at the menu.

"You want I come back?" the waitress said, lowering her pad and pen.

"No, he's going to order now," Kat said firmly.

"OK, OK," said Marty, turning back to the first page. "Uh…sizzling rice soup is chicken, right?"

"Yes, very good," the waitress said, writing this down.

"No, then, what about the hot and sour soup? It's fish, right?"

"Yes, very good," said the waitress, scratching out her previous entry.

"OK, hot and sour soup."

"For two?" said the waitress, writing in Chinese.

"Please," said Marty, turning a page in the menu. "Is the garlic-sauce eggplant good?"

"Everything good," said the waitress, glancing at another table that looked ready for their check.

"All right, the eggplant and…mushu pork." He looked up at Kat. "For me, OK?"

"You want rice?" asked the waitress.

"Uh, yeah, sure," said Marty, putting down his menu.

"Fried or steamed?" asked the waitress.

Marty was a trapped animal. "God, um, the fried has pork, right?"

"Yes, very good," said the waitress.

"She doesn't eat meat," said Marty.

"Only little meat," said the waitress.

"Uh, steamed will be fine," said Marty. "And no MSG, OK?"

"That what give it good flavor," said the waitress, taking his empty beer bottle.

"Yeah, well, that what gives me good headache," said Marty.

The waitress shrugged, collected their menus and headed towards the other table to see if they were done.

"I can't believe you had another accident," said Marty. He took a swallow of beer.

"You had one," she said.

"It wasn't my fault."

"So you assume it was my fault," said Kat, finishing her wine.

"Was it?" said Marty.

"I don't know, I guess," said Kat, wishing she'd asked the waitress for another glass of wine as she disappeared into the kitchen.

"You zoned out, didn't you?"

"I can't remember, it happened so fast."

"You went to Katland."

…The biting wind whipped her thick hair across her face as it cut through the thin rayon of her knee-length print dress. Marty, fedora low on his forehead and hands jammed into the pockets of his trench coat, searched her eyes. "I mean, half the time I don't even know who I'm talking to," he said.

"Whom," corrected Kat, huddling against the cold as the fog rolled across the runway.

"Whatever," said Marty.

"Sorry, I know that drives you crazy," she said.

A motor on the silver DC-3 lurking behind them in the fog coughed to life, ta-pocketa-pocketa-pocketa-pocketa-pocketa, then caught on with a huge roar, blades cutting the frigid air.

"I'm way past crazy," said Marty. "Last night we said a great many things. You said I was to do the thinking for both of us."

The second motor on the plane coughed and sputtered, then roared to life, and the sleek silver aircraft shuddered, restless for the sky.

"Well, I've done a lot of it since then, and it all adds up to one thing: you're getting on that plane with Victor where you belong," Marty said earnestly.

"But, Marty, no, I…

"Now, you've got to listen to me! You have any idea what you'd have to look forward to if you stayed here?

Nine chances out of ten, we'd both wind up in a concentration camp." He took the half-smoked cigarette from his lips and flipped it into the night as if he were facing a firing squad.

"That's why I think maybe we should take a break"...

Kat stared at Marty's lips, moving in slow motion.

"Earth to Kat!" he said.

"What?"

"Did you hear anything I said?"

"Absolutely," said Kat as the waitress arrived at the table with their food. "You said you want to break up."

"No, take a break. I said we need to take a break."

"Hot and sour soup," said the waitress.

"In other words, you can't make up your mind whether you want to be with me or not. Or maybe you want to break up, but you just can't say it?"

"Garlic sauce eggplant?" Kat raised her hand without taking her eyes off Marty, and the waitress put the plate in front of her.

"Maybe, I don't know," said Marty, as the waitress gave him his mushu pork.

"Maybe Marty," said Kat.

"God, I hate it when you say that," he said, getting mad.

"More drinks?" the waitress said hopefully.

§

Marty parked his car in front of Kat's apartment, leaving the engine running.

"Why are you so angry?" he said.

"Are you crazy?" she sputtered, "you just dumped me!"

"I didn't dump you, I said I wanted to take a break. I honestly thought you'd be OK with it. All you seem to care about is your job."

"Like your job isn't important?"

"I try to have a life," he said, "at least a real one."

Kat threw the car door open. "I can't do this anymore," she said, getting out.

"Wait," Marty said plaintively. "I didn't want it to be like this."

"What the hell did you expect?"

"I don't know. Friendlier?"

"Perfect," said Kat. "Well, it's friendly, Marty. That's all it's been for a long time."

"What do you mean?" he said lamely.

"You went to graduate school. Figure it out." She slammed the car door, knowing he would wince at the sound, then stomped across the lawn. He drove away before she reached the glass doors to the lobby, and she turned and watched his taillights disappear.

Suddenly weighed down with sadness, Kat entered the lobby and walked to the elevator, then remembered its urine-soaked carpet, which wouldn't be taken care of until she said something to the super. *What a royally fucked up day.* She took a deep breath and entered the stairwell, barely managing to hold it until she reached her floor, gasping as she entered the hallway and walked to her door. It took her a moment to find her keys and her hand was shaking as she unlocked the door.

Inside, she leaned against the door for a moment surveying her apartment, the boxes of books, the empty wine glass and bottle, the shoes she'd worn to work that day, then started bawling. Tears streaming down her cheeks, she went into the tiny kitchenette and twisted the oven knob to 325°, then found the Billie Holiday CD from one of the stacks on a side table, inserted it into the player, and *A Fine Romance* filled the room. Her phone was in her purse. She speed dialed. When the call was answered loud Techno nearly drowned out Tina's voice.

"Silly me, I was afraid I'd wake you," said Kat, sniffling.

"It's only eleven-thirty," shouted Tina.

"Yeah, well, it's a school night." Kat dabbed her eyes with a relatively clean dish towel.

"I finished my homework. Are you OK?"

"Yeah...no. Marty broke up with me."

"'Maybe' Marty broke up with you?" said an incredulous Tina.

"Wonders never cease," muttered Kat.

"What?" shouted Tina.

"Nothing," said Kat.

"You want I come over? I can be there in, like, a half hour," shouted Tina.

"No, I'm OK. I just wanted to…look, I'm OK," said Kat. "Really."

"You sure?"

"Yeah, I'm sure," mumbled Kat.

"What?" shouted Tina over the din of the nightclub Kat knew was jammed with disturbingly thin, ultra-stylish twenty-something Asians.

"I'll see you tomorrow," Kat said loudly.

"OK," shouted Tina, "we'll talk in the morning. I'll bring the coffee. Take care of you."

Kat put her phone on the counter and returned to the tiny kitchenette. Tiny, but it had a good oven—it had already reached 300°. She opened cupboards to find flour, brown sugar, baking soda, salt, bourbon vanilla, eggs and rich dark chocolate. Blue-glazed bowl, long wooden spoon. She folded the vanilla into melted butter, and the memory curtain parted slightly. Cold buttered-pan, chocolate-studded drops swelled in the hot oven, filling the room with scent, now mixed with nostalgic cologne, rustling skirts, a gentle hand on her back, encouraging. Always such nice shoes for everyday.

three

Kat woke with the same scent of chocolate chip cookies and sense of peace she'd felt when she'd fallen asleep. She picked up her phone, its clock reading 5:55 AM, preemptively turned off the alarm, and scrolled through the flurry of East Coast email. And the day intruded. Then, with the fresh clarity of her mental vacation, she made decisions. She'd wasted eight years on Marty. Never again. From now on if someone didn't have at least one princely quality he was out of there. She was such a bad driver it was amazing she'd lived this long. She'd return the rental and take the bus until the MINI was fixed, then sell it and take the bus and subway. There was probably a schedule online. It was crazy to agree to join Jason's "team," she was having trouble handling the workload she had now, and Rebecca was already on her about it. And speaking of Rebecca, she had to say something to Tina about her weird new work ethic of not working, or her friend was going to be out of a job. Two sheets of cookies greeted her when she padded into the kitchenette. She ate one as she watched her espresso maker chugging on the burner.

§

The bus that dropped Kat two blocks from her office had been surprisingly comfortable, but had taken longer than estimated; she'd definitely need to allow more time. They hadn't been surprised at the auto repair shop when she returned the rental, but the girl at the counter had given it an especially irritating looking over before signing off on it, like she couldn't believe Kat could have it for one day without at least putting a ding in it. Kat offered Jack a cookie from the lightly grease-stained box, but Scorpion Nails got none.

Late now, Kat hurried up the stairs to her building, her laptop and purse over one shoulder, the cookies in her free hand. The glass doors hissed open and she entered the granite corridor, pausing at the security desk to open the cookie box so Gus could help himself.

"You OK?" he said, regarding the overstuffed box.

"I'm fine," said Kat, wondering why he'd ask that. "I'm also late."

"Sorry," said Gus, finally choosing one fairly bursting with chocolate chips.

Kat got on the elevator, holding the door for a woman she recognized from accounting, who looked at the cookie box and said, "God, those smell amazing, what are they?"

"Cookies."

"Where did you get them?"

"I made them, actually," Kat said, opening the box.

§

Kat left the cookies in the lunchroom, not taking the time to get coffee because she was worried about Rebecca. She managed to rip through seven emails before the rolling Windows blue screen of death seized her computer. "Oh, for the love of God," she said, rebooting. She leaned back in her chair and looked at the whistling air vent above her desk as her computer whirred.

Tina hurried in on her way to her cubicle, stopping to deposit a Starbucks bag on Kat's desk, with a quick "Morning."

"Good morning," said Kat. "You just missed Rebecca."

"Shit," said Tina quietly on the other side of the wall.

"Kidding."

"That was mean," said Tina.

"No, that was a friendly warning. You don't want to be a chink in her chain."

Tina's head popped over the divider. "Did you just call me a 'Chink'?

"Yeah, right," said Kat, logging on to her computer. "Virulent racist that I am." She looked back up at the air vent. "Do you ever imagine poison is coming out of that vent?"

Juanita appeared in Kat's doorway. "Doll, those cookies are beyond amazing."

"You brought cookies?" said Tina.

"Chocolate chip," said Kat, confirming her password.

"They're like sex without the wet spot," said Juanita.

"There's a visual I could have lived without," said Kat, re-opening the email she'd been working on before the system crash.

"So, do we need to talk?" said Tina.

"Talk? About what?" said Juanita, her nose for news twitching.

"Marty broke up with her last night."

"Maybe Marty broke up with you?" marveled Juanita.

"I still have twenty-seven emails to respond to and a summary due before noon, and this effing computer keeps crashing. The Marty saga will have to wait till lunch."

"You got it," said Juanita. She looked up at Tina. "Stuckie was looking for you."

"For real?"

"Uh, yeah," said Juanita.

"When?"

"A half hour ago?"

"Shit," said Tina. "Did she ask about the Roth report?"

"I gave it to her after you left yesterday," said Kat. "Told her you asked me to proof it."

"Thanks, GF," said Tina. "I owe you one."

"More than one," scoffed Juanita, disappearing down the aisle.

"Fortunately I'm not counting," said Kat, "but think about what I said."

"Right," said Tina. "Don't be a chink. That's good advice."

§

Kat, Tina and Juanita met for lunch at a bustling mid-town burger joint. Ensconced in a red vinyl booth, Kat and Tina had chopped salads, Juanita a double-cheeseburger with fries, all of which she salted heavily.

"I'm amazed he actually made a decision," said Kat, liberally peppering her salad.

"He's so calling you back," said Tina, looking for the waitress with her iced tea.

"I don't know, in a way I'm kind of relieved," said Kat. "It was like the relationship was on autopilot."

"How long were you together?" said Juanita, flooding her plate with catsup.

"Eight years."

"Jesus, I was in the ninth grade," said Tina.

"Thank you for that," said Kat.

"The lovin' must have been good," said Juanita, salting the hell out of everything on her plate again before taking a huge bite of her hamburger.

"Not really," said Kat. "It's been 'event sex' since about the second year. You know, birthday sex, anniversary sex, vacation sex, or after a party if he saw someone really hot. I could always tell when I was the proxy." She looked at Tina. "Like after we had dinner with you the first time?"

"What are you saying?" said Tina.

"That he was probably thinking about you when he was, you know, doing it with me."

"Gross," said Tina, finally catching the waitress' eye.

"Anyway, it was more like we were pals," Kat said wistfully.

"Well, I don't know how you did it," said Juanita. "I couldn't live without Boo's voodoo."

"I gotta' say I never got it," said Tina. "You're like Ms. Romance. Plus, you're hot, and Marty's, um…"

"Not?" finished Juanita.

"Well, yeah," said Tina.

"I guess I figured he was safe, you know? That he'd always be there."

"You mean when you got home from work?" said Tina, as the waitress finally brought her iced tea.

"Are you implying that I'm job-obsessed?" sniffed Kat.

"No way," said Tina, tearing the paper off the straw.

"OK, maybe a little. Sometimes it feels like it's the only constant in my life besides Katland."

"Is that a TV show?" said Juanita.

"It's what Marty calls my imagination. Not a compliment." Kat picked at her salad. "Do you think it can ever be like in our dreams?"

"Uh, no. That's why they call them dreams," said Tina.

Kat's phone vibrated in her purse. She got it out and checked the caller ID. "No idea who this is," she said, answering it.

Juanita and Tina watched her say "Kat Young," then have a brief conversation culminating in her writing down a phone number. After she ended the call she stared at the phone for a moment.

"Everything OK?" said Tina.

"My aunt died."

"Wow, sorry," said Tina.

"Oh, honey," said Juanita.

"I haven't seen her since I was, like, eight. Weird, my mother didn't say anything about it when she called me yesterday. But maybe she doesn't know; they had some kind of major falling out." Kat put the phone back in her purse, still processing her news. "Aunt Ruth left me her house."

§

Tina insisted on driving, even though Kat had said she needed to get used to the bus. It was the second day in a row she'd left work at five, and it felt weird to be out with the rest of the drones when she'd usually be hunkered down in her cubicle for at least another two hours.

"You never would have made it on time to meet the realtor taking the bus," said Tina, piloting "Daisy," her yellow VW, through the rush-hour traffic.

"You're right, thanks," Kat said, looking at the plastic daisy in the little vase attached to the dashboard. The car also had white daisy-shaped wheels with yellow centers. Tina definitely had style.

But Kat wasn't sure she was ready to talk to the realtor, who had been waiting for the results of Ruth's will because she had a buyer who wanted the house. Kat had agreed to meet her mostly to get her off the phone because she had IT in her office dealing with her software issues and a regional manager on hold. She needed time to process everything, but time was something she never seemed to have enough of.

"It's been so long, none of this was here," said Kat. "I think you turn right at the corner of that mini-mall, then it's, like, half a block down." She noted a bus bench near the intersection. "There's a handy bus stop."

"There's nothing handy about a bus," said Tina, making the turn. "But there is a fueling station," she said, indicating the Starbucks anchoring the strip-mall.

The little yellow car with the daisy wheels rolled down the quiet tree-lined side street of post-war bungalows. "That's it," said Kat, pointing to a pretty little Craftsman, in disrepair amid a weed-filled yard. Tina pulled over to the curb beneath a towering Jacaranda that had spread a snowy blanket of purple blossoms. She shut off the engine, and they looked at the house quietly for a moment.

"You have a house," said Tina, breaking the silence. "You're, like, a grownup."

"I wouldn't go that far," said Kat, experiencing a whirl of emotions. If a house could have a spirit, this one was welcoming her. But there was something else there, a strange anxiety.

"Well, come on then," said Tina, climbing out of Daisy, and Kat followed her to the porch, where she used the key to her new house for the first time. She opened the door and they stepped tentatively into the dank, musty air, tinged with something else, something she knew instantly to be her aunt's illness. The plaster walls were cracked and water stained, the carpet stained as well, but more uncertainly.

"Pew," said Tina, "you might want to leave the windows open for a few years."

"It used to be so lovely," said Kat. "I guess she was pretty sick at the end."

She walked across the room and looked into the grimy kitchen.

"I loved coming here when I was a kid; I always thought she had a nicer house than ours."

"I can't believe that smell," said Tina, grimacing at a suspicious dark spot on the carpet. "What's that stain?"

"I don't think we want to know," said Kat. She knelt and pulled up a corner of the carpet. "At least there's nice wood underneath."

Tina walked down the hall to the master bedroom. Kat followed and looked over her shoulder. There was a walnut four-poster bed, dresser, and a vanity with a stool padded in tattered velvet. An ornate music box sat on the vanity, surrounded by dozens of perfume bottles. Tina picked up a Lalique perfume bottle and sniffed it, then lifted the lid on the music box and a bell-like *Somewhere My Love* filled the room.

"Cool," said Tina.

"I loved that when I was a little girl," said Kat looking sadly at the bed's stained mattress. "It's sad to think she died alone. I'm so pissed at my mother for not telling me."

Tina sniffed a Hermès bottle. "Do you know how much this shit costs?"

"It used to drive my mother crazy that Ruth could afford that, while we were shopping at Sear's and Penny's. One day we were playing with makeup and my mother showed up and dragged me out, screaming at Ruth like a maniac. I was howling my head off in the car as she scrubbed my face with a wad of tissues, which, of course, she spit on."

"Sounds like a Jerry Springer episode," said Tina.

"It was definitely an episode. Ruth didn't say a word, just stood there and watched us drive away, looking so sad."

"Hello?" The woman's voice came from the front of the house.

Kat went to the bedroom door and saw Jacqueline Ross, a forty-something medically-sculptured blond wearing a tight blazer, skinny jeans, heels and a great deal of jewelry, at the front door. "Ms. Young? I'm Jacqueline Ross, your realtor?" she said.

"Come in," said Kat, not quite ready for the "your realtor" part.

"So, have you had a chance to make a decision?" Jacqueline said, looking Tina up and down.

"No, I'm sorry. This has all been so sudden. It's the first time I've seen the house in twenty years."

"I understand, but I do have a highly motivated buyer, and they don't grow on trees these days."

"No shit," said Tina.

Jacqueline regarded her again, suspiciously, then fished in her purse for a pen. "If I could have my card back for a moment?" Kat returned the card and Jacqueline wrote a dollar amount on it and gave it back to her.

"Wow," said Kat.

"Exactly," said Jacqueline. "Considering the condition of the house, it's a wonderful offer." She dropped her pen back in her purse as Tina took the card from Kat's fingers.

"Holy shit," said Tina, earning her another look from Jacqueline.

"All righty, then," said Jacqueline, efficiently finishing up their meeting. "My buyer is looking at another property, but right now your house is his preferred choice. Let me know ASAP what you want to do." She snapped her bag shut. "Lovely to meet you both," she said, this last bit without looking at Tina. In truth, Jacqueline couldn't say the word "shit" if she had a mouth full, nor did she especially like hearing it used in conversation.

Kat closed the door behind her.

"All righty, then," said Tina, returning the card.

Kat looked at it again. "It is a lot of money."

"You could probably even afford car insurance," said Tina.

"Very funny. I'm riding the bus. It isn't just about the money. I'm a menace."

"So, do you want to get some dinner?"

"I think I'm going to hang here for a while. Think about this."

"Soak in the vibe," said Tina.

"It does smell pretty bad."

"Are you gonna' be OK? I mean, like, to get home?"

"Like I said, I need to get used to the bus. But thanks for, you know, driving."

"No problem, I'll see you tomorrow," Tina said, tottering out the door on her impossibly tall shoes. She turned at the top stair. "It's really nice. I mean, it doesn't smell that bad."

"Yes it does," smiled Kat. "But it has good bones. See you tomorrow."

She closed the door and turned to the room. "Talk to me, house, what should I do?" But any house spirits were quiet. She pulled open the curtains, thick with dust, and the soft evening light bathed the room. She looked back into the kitchen, the porcelain O'Keefe & Merritt gas stove thick with grease, the sink chipped and stained, more dirt than grout between the tile on the counters and floor.

Kat wandered into the bedroom and pulled the drapes apart, sneezing from the dust. She sat down in front of the little army of sculptured perfume bottles, sniffing each thoughtfully. She opened a drawer and brought out a black enameled lipstick tube, slid the cap off and leaned into the mirror, carefully describing the arc of her lips with the deep, almost violent red. She turned the music box over and wound the key, then lifted the lid, and *Somewhere My Love* filled the room.

§

Kat locked the door, stopping at the end of the walk to look back at the little house in the deepening shadows. Besides the Jacaranda there was a Pepper Tree, its willow-like branches promising shade and Christmassy red berries, and what appeared to be a very mature citrus tree. Lemon? She couldn't remember.

She turned and walked toward the bus stop, the sidewalk and parked cars covered with a lush carpet of purple flowers from the Jacarandas lining the street. *No problem, no car.* At the corner she put her laptop and purse on the bench, feeling a strange kind of peace, the first she remembered in years. No sign of the bus. She looked back at the Starbucks, and saw a perfect (except for a crumpled left rear fender) bright red 1949 GMC pickup parked right in front.

She tried to see who was at the tables or waiting for the cashier, but her view was obscured by the parked cars. She turned back to the street. The bus was coming. *What the hell, he drove off.* She looked back at the pickup truck's mangled fender. She sighed, picked up her laptop and purse and crossed the parking lot.

When she reached the door of the coffee shop she saw him, clearly the same guy, even dressed the same, except it was a tail-out T-shirt over well-worn jeans, waiting as the world's most indecisive Starbuck's customer stumbled through his order. She took her place at the end of the line as the guy in front squinted at the list on the wall.

"Uh, a triple Grande half-caff two percent pumpkin spice latte…" He leaned over the bakery case. "…and a whole wheat no-sugar-added pumpkin mini loaf."

Unable to resist the need to share the moment, the pickup owner looked back at Kat. "Wasn't this a Saturday Night Live sketch?" he said quietly.

The barista placed a lid and sleeve on a cup of steaming coffee. "Caffé Americano, black as night," she said, setting it on the counter beside the register, and the pickup owner walked over to her, taking out his wallet.

"That's two dollars," she said, ringing up the sale. He gave her the money, picked up his coffee and turned to leave, but looked at Kat again. "Have we met before?" he said. "I'm not trying to, you know…you just look familiar."

Kat hesitated, feeling shy and tongue-tied on top of the awkwardness of the whole accident thing. "I, uh…I'm not sure. I just moved here. I mean, not, you know, here, not into Starbucks…" *My God, what am I saying?* "Like, a block away?"

"Cool," he said, "welcome to the neighborhood."

He pushed the door open to leave, giving her a parting smile.

"Wait," said Kat, walking over to him. "Actually, we have met." She pointed to his mangled fender. "I put that dent in your truck."

"So that was you, without your..." he indicated his face.

"Airbag powder and hysteria," said Kat.

"Wow. OK. So..."

"Look, I feel terrible, you left before I could give you my insurance."

"Don't worry about it. I'm not," he said, pushing the door open.

"Well, that's nice enough to be weird, but I want to do the right thing. She fished in her purse for a pen and business card. "Here's my office number, and my cell," she said, writing on the card. "Please, get an estimate and I'll take care of it."

"OK..." he said, looking at the card, "...Kat." He extended his hand, "I'm Cooper. It was nice running into you in a less violent manner."

Kat, used to being the one doling out the sarcasm, shook his hand awkwardly, and answered his parting smile as he pushed through the door. Behind her, the barista said, "Can I help you?"

four

...Kat pressed her back against the soft leather of the sofa in Jason's office, penciling notes on a yellow legal pad as they discussed their plans for the project. Still on the emotional rollercoaster of the week, she tried to put her burgeoning feelings for this amazing man out of her head, focusing all her energy on the task at hand.

"We'll want Starkovitch, Bradley and Cohen on board," he said, his back to her as he surveyed the traffic twenty stories below. He turned to her. "If you could try to set something up for later in the month?"

"No problem," said Kat, jotting this down. "Have you considered the Qualtech consortium as a potential partner?" She said, looking up at him. "If we could combine our product with their distribution channels the others will be begging to sign on."

Jason's jaw literally dropped. "That's brilliant. I can't believe no one's thought of that before."

"Just seemed logical," said Kat modestly.

"No," said Jason, "it's more than logic, more than reason." The moment froze in time, Jason backlit, god-like, the air between them wafting a faint scent of verbena and cedar and fine wool. "God, you have beautiful eyes," he said and she put the legal pad and pencil aside and returned his gaze unafraid, fully sensing the inevitability of what was about to happen and the futility of resistance. In a mere moment he would be beside her and she in his arms, sharing the most intense kiss two lovers have ever shared in the history of the world. Yet Kat turned her head away, struggling to maintain the magic of the moment in spite of the overwhelming stench, feeling her world crumbling. "You got great boobs. Sweet" he said, his breath fetid…

Kat pressed against the wall of the bus to put as much distance as possible between herself and the huge filthy man who had collapsed into the seat next to her.

"Ever think of taking a bath, *pendejo*?" the tatted-up kid seated behind them said as he jumped to his feet, relocating to the aisle at the front of the crowded bus.

"People in LA have such bad manners," the guy muttered.

Kat risked looking at him. He wasn't that big after all; he was just wearing everything he owned.

"Some people think it's bad manners not to bathe," she said.

"You mean, like, in the bathroom?" he said fiercely enough she regretted speaking to him.

"Uh, that's where people usually bathe," she said, digging herself in deeper.

"I guess they left that out WHEN THEY BUILT MY CARDBOARD BOX!" he screamed at her.

"Oh, right," said Kat, aware that all eyes were on them now, including the driver's, via his mirror. "Sorry, I…"

An explosive belch erupted from somewhere beneath the whiskers and grime.

"Man," he said, swallowing hard, "ever get one of those burps where you can taste your whole entire breakfast in the order you ate it in?"

"Oh…my…God," said Kat, trying to become as small as possible in the corner of her seat.

"So, I'll give you twenty bucks," he said suavely, his attention returning to her breasts.

"For what?" said Kat, calculating her escape.

"Sex," he answered, surprised she had to ask. "What else would I give you twenty bucks for?"

Kat looked him in squarely in the eye. "Show me."

"What?" he said, confused.

"The twenty. Show me the money."

"Well, you know…"

"That's what I thought," she said, gathering her things and pushing herself to her feet. "Excuse me, this is my stop."

"OK, so I'm temporarily financially embarrassed," he said as she squeezed by his heavily padded knees. "I can get it by Tuesday."

"Sorry, no money, no sex, that's the way the world works." As she reached the aisle the people in the adjoining seats applauded. She stopped, turned, and lifted her hands to them in a slight bow that said, "Thank you, my degradation is complete."

Kat made it to the front of the bus just as it reached her stop. The driver looked up at her as he opened the door and said, "Every day." She stepped down to the street, her birthday beginning pretty much as expected.

§

The first thing Kat saw when she entered her cubicle was the balloons floating above her computer, a half-dozen, silver Mylar, printed "Happy 30!!!," although they may have just as well have shouted "Made In China!!!" It had to be Tina, her extreme youth comfortably insulating her from that birthday. She put the bag with the coffee and croissant she'd bought on her desk next to her monitor, and her purse and laptop on the chair in the corner, then sat down and turned on her computer. Waiting for it to boot, she glanced at the balloons again and shook her head. She picked up the phone and dialed. It rang four times, then she heard the familiar voice, "This is Jean, I'm sorry I missed you but your message is very important to me so please leave a message when you have heard the beep sound and I will return your call," followed by some fumbling as her mother had sorted out which button to push to end it and, FINALLY, the beep. Cursing caller ID, Kat said, "Mom, I know you're there, you're always there. I really need to talk to you."

Her phone vibrated in her purse and she got it out and saw "Marty Kaplan" on the screen. Thinking *That didn't last long,* she dropped her phone back into her purse. He could just stew a little longer. She leaned back and looked at the balloons. What did she really want for her birthday?

...*"Wow, congratulations."* She turned and Jason was smiling in her doorway. *"You should have taken the day."*

"I couldn't even think of it. I'm so behind as it is."

"Something special planned for tonight?" he ventured.

"This is one of those birthdays I'd rather forget."

"C'mon, you're gonna' make me feel old," he said, grinning. *"Let me buy you dinner. I promise not to talk about work."* One of his bicuspids actually sparkled...

Kat tugged on a balloon string and it bounced in the air. A romance with one of her boss's superiors would be crazy. On the other hand, the only solid offer she'd had recently was from a guy who had apparently given up bathing. She booted up her laptop and opened the "Peterson Project" file, then untied one of the balloons and walked up the aisle to the elevators.

§

Jason's office was on the top floor, next to the CEO's. As she got off the elevator and walked toward his door, a secretary passed her carrying a dozen file folders, a disturbingly thin (for her large breast size) young woman wearing a tight white cotton blouse over an even tighter short straight black skirt, and teetering on ridiculously (for a work environment) high heels. Kat reached Jason's closed door and knocked lightly.

The girl said, "Jason isn't here today. He had a family emergency," adding, "nice balloon," before disappearing into one of the offices at the end of the hall.

Kat wasn't sure what bothered her more, that she'd referred to him by his first name, the buttons pulling on the front of her shirt, or her remark about the balloon.

When she got back to her desk she shut down her laptop, then opened her email. She wished she could take the day; she was having trouble concentrating. She looked at her purse, then took out her phone. *This had better be good*, she thought as she speed dialed Marty's number.

"Marty Kaplan."

Doesn't he have caller ID? "It's Kat."

"Hey, how you doin'?" he said.

"Great, thanks! Did you call to ask me that?"

"No, I feel bad. I didn't handle, you know, *that* well."

"No kidding," said Kat. "Also no surprise. What do you want, Marty?"

"There's something I need to talk to you about."

"So talk," said Kat.

"I'd rather do it in person. Can I see you after work?" Marty said, a slight whine entering his voice. "I'm trying to do things right for a change."

Kat wanted to say she needed more time, but when she answered him it was like she was listening to someone else speaking. "Whatever. There's a Starbucks at Olympic and Overland," she said, naming the shop near her aunt's house. She assumed he wanted to talk

63

about them living together. He could see the house. "I can be there at six thirty."

"Don't you want to meet somewhere near work or your apartment?"

She was starting to get annoyed. Had he really forgotten it was her birthday? "That's where I want to meet. If it's a problem, maybe we should just forget it." Kat checked herself and lowered her voice so everyone on the floor wouldn't hear her screaming at her stupid boyfriend. "In fact, know what, that's a good idea, let's just forget it."

Marty quickly said, "It's OK. I'll see you there. Bye."

As Kat tossed her phone on her desk, Juanita appeared in her doorway. "We still getting drinks tonight, Three-O Girl?"

"Tell me you didn't do this," said Kat, indicating the balloons.

"None other, girlfriend," said Juanita. "Jumpstart the party."

"Happy thirty? You really think I want to be reminded of that?"

"Hey, I'd love to see thirty again. So, where we goin' for those birthday Cosmos?"

"Oh, I thought I told you, I'm going over to my mother's place. She got a cake or something," Kat said, not ready to talk about the Marty development.

"And here Boo give me the night off and everything. Well, we at least buyin' you a birthday lunch," said Juanita, heading back to her work station.

"Sure," Kat said after her. "I'll come and get you." She turned back to her email, but someone cleared his throat in her doorway. She looked up. It was Max, her

IT guy. If Max were a musician, his nerdy look (bleached multi-directional hair, horn-rimmed glasses, light blue short-sleeve shirt with three pens and a small clipped-on screwdriver in the pocket, and too-short chinos over tan chukka boots) would be cool. But Max wasn't a musician.

"Good morning, Max," Kat said sweetly, returning her attention to the screen.

"Good morning," said Max, cautiously gauging her mood.

"How are things among the Droid folk?" she said, finishing an email.

"You know what day it is," said Max, bumping his messenger bag against his leg.

"Thursday?" Kat said, hitting send and opening another pointless message from a prematurely-promoted district manager.

"Security settings day."

"Are you sure?"

"Yes, it's Thursday. I check security settings on Thursday. You know that," said Max.

"What I know is I have fifty emails to answer and a project due by five that a normal person, one without my super-powers, couldn't finish by next Thursday at five."

"Well, I have fifty more stations to do," Max said hopelessly.

Kat finally turned her chair and looked at him. "So do them."

"They have to be in order."

"You really have to do them in order, or it's one of your OCD things?"

Max's eyes narrowed, his mouth tightened. "That's mean," he said.

"Mean? You have no idea." Kat grabbed her stapler, opened it and turned it on him. "Go away, or I'll staple you."

"Are you crazy?" he said.

"Crazy? Do I look crazy to you?"

"A little," said Max. He looked at the doorway to Tina's cubicle, thinking, *Shit.*

§

"I can't believe you guys; this place is expensive," Kat said looking around the chic restaurant as Tina and Juanita studied their menus. Most of the patrons were in black, and half of them were wearing their sunglasses indoors.

Juanita put her menu down and took a sip of water. "Can't wait to tell Boo I'm drinking ten dollar water." She squinted across the room. "Is that Jennifer Anniston?"

"You think every cute white girl is Jennifer Anniston," said Tina, not even bothering to look.

"I don't think Kat looks like Jennifer Anniston," said Juanita, still staring at the woman, who was picking at a crab salad.

"Thanks," said Kat.

"Seriously, I think it's her," said Juanita as their server arrived at the table.

"Have you decided?" the young woman asked.

"Birthday girl goes first," said Juanita.

"I'll have the seared tuna salad," said Kat, "and no cake or singing, please."

"No problem," said the server, "anyone singing Happy Birthday is immediately asked to leave."

Kat studied her face for signs she was kidding as she turned to Juanita.

"I want a burger, please," said Juanita.

"How do you want it cooked?" asked the server, smoothing her apron against her black slacks. "Rare? Medium? Well?"

"<u>Well</u>," said Juanita, "I want the moo out that thing. Does it come with fries? It don't say nothin' about fries on the menu."

"Shoestring, very crispy," said the young woman. "They're dangerously delicious."

"That's what I want," said Juanita. "A burger with dangerous fries. And lots of ketchup."

"Sorry, chef doesn't allow it," she said, turning to Tina.

"What?" said Juanita, giving the word two full syllables.

"Chef has precisely designed every flavor of every dish served at Pomposo, and no condiments are allowed," the server patiently explained. She returned her attention to Tina. "Your decision?"

Tina looked back at her menu. "Sushi—maguro, crunchy roll and…uni."

"Very good," the girl said.

Tina put her finger on another menu item. "How's the spider roll?"

"Everything at Pomposo is perfect," the server said somberly.

"Then I'll have one of those too. And a bottle of the Conundrum."

"Very good," said the server. "Do you want another bottle of Pellegrino?"

"We're OK," said Tina.

"Wine on a school day?" Kat said, as their server returned to the kitchen.

"Wine on your birthday," said Tina.

"Yeah, especially since we don't get to have Cosmos tonight," said Juanita.

"Yeah, what's up with that?" said Tina. "You're really going to your mother's house on your birthday?"

"Yes, I'm really going," lied Kat.

"Alone, to your mother's house, without one of us along so you have to actually talk to her?" said Tina, suspicious.

"Yes, alone."

"How are you getting there?" Tina asked, still not satisfied.

"The way I get everywhere now, on the bus."

"Don't know how you do it," said Juanita. "Getting around in LA is bad enough."

"It's OK. I can read, work on my laptop, think, not kill anyone with my car. To say nothing of the social opportunities. You wouldn't believe the offer I had this morning."

"You met someone on the bus?" said Juanita.

"Yeah, but he was overdressed and underfunded."

The server arrived with their wine. Kat had taken an instant dislike to her, reinforced by the whole catsup deal with Juanita. "Who's tasting?" she asked.

Kat said, "I'm sure it's fine; you can just pour it."

The girl did so, leaving them with, "I'll be right back with your entrées."

"To my dearest friends," Kat said, lifting her glass.

"We got your back," said Juanita as she and Tina met Kat's glass with their own. "Now we just got to find you a <u>real</u> man."

"I don't know, maybe Marty wasn't so bad," said Kat.

"You just said 'maybe Marty,'" Tina pointed out.

"Maybe this is the time to rethink the game plan," Kat continued.

"You have a game plan?" wondered Tina.

"I have a game plan," said Kat. Her eyes narrowed. "You don't think I have a game plan?"

"Not that I've noticed," said Tina. She looked at Juanita. "You see a game plan?"

"No game or plan," said Juanita.

"Rescue, that's the dream, right?" said Tina, refilling Kat's glass.

"I could use a rescue from the rescue," said Juanita.

"But realistically, am I rescue material?" said Kat. "I mean, I'm sarcastic as hell, average looking…"

"You have big boobs," said Tina, "guys will sell their parents to al-Qaeda for a nice rack."

"That's so true," said Juanita, tasting the wine cautiously. "Boo does love mine. We take a shower together, these babies get clean," she said, creating another two syllable word with "clean."

"Yeah, but Kat's skinny. Skinny with big boobs is, like, the Holy Grail of guydom."

"Thank you for that," said Kat, noting the approach of the server with their lunches and hoping they were done with the topic.

"Well, I wish I could eat like you eat and look the way you look," said Juanita.

"I don't eat that much," said Kat.

"That's what I mean," said Juanita anticipating her burger and dangerous fries.

§

When Kat got back to work she wondered how she was going to be able to finish the day, having drunk almost half the bottle of wine (Juanita didn't finish her first glass). Feeling drowsy as she waited for the elevator, she replayed the morning, prioritizing. She still had at least a hundred emails to answer, and Rebecca was waiting for her project report. Then she remembered Max calling her "mean" and felt a twinge of guilt. Kat didn't just pride herself on being a kind person, she was, and being stressed out of her mind was no excuse. When she got on the elevator she pressed the button for the IT floor.

When the doors opened and Kat stepped off, the first thing she noticed was how quiet it was. Having never deigned to set foot on Max's floor, she assumed it would be buzzing with telephone conversations the same as any other open cubicle floor. As she went down the aisle, checking the names posted by each doorway, she saw quiet men and women tapping away at keyboards, eyes glued to their screens. She asked a skinny Asian guy with spiky hair and an armload of printouts which space was Max Neufeld's.

"It's that one," he said pointing to a cubicle at the end of the next row, "but he's up in accounting dealing with a crash."

"That's OK," said Kat, "I just want to leave him a note."

"Maybe that's not such a great idea," the guy said, looking uncomfortable.

"It's OK, he knows me," Kat said, adding, "thanks," as she walked towards it.

"No problem," said the guy, turning to watch her.

At first Kat didn't notice the photos on the wall behind the monitor in Max's office because she was looking for a Post-It pad to leave her apology on. It was when she sat down to write it that she saw them: a dozen candid snapshots of herself, at her desk, in the lunchroom and the lobby and several on the street near their building. *Oh, dear.* She crumpled the Post-It and dropped it in the wastebasket by the door on her way out.

When Kat passed the Asian tech's cubicle he said, "Ms. Young," and she stopped, although she really didn't feel like talking about Max's photo montage.

"You saw the pictures?" he said from his cubicle's doorway.

"Uh, yeah."

"Kinda' weird."

"Pretty much," said Kat. "You know, I should get back to my desk, I have all this work."

"It's not like he's a dangerous stalker or something, he just really likes you."

Kat thought about this, then said, "I like him too. I mean, he's strange, but he seems like a nice kid. I've got to think about this." She started to leave, then stopped to add, "Don't tell him I was here, OK?"

The techie said, "OK."

She pushed the button for the elevator, then looked back and the guy was still looking at her. "I see what he means about you," he said.

"What's that?" said Kat.

"That you're the nicest person he deals with."

"That's a frightening thought," said Kat as the elevator doors opened.

§

By the time she reached her desk, Kat had decided not to call HR about Max's hobby, knowing he'd probably be fired immediately. *We're all crazy*, she thought. *But it isn't acceptable and I have to talk to him about it.* The phone on her desk rang as she was waking her computer. She regarded it as an alien object, as if she were a native of an Amazon rain forest tribe who had been completely sheltered from modern technology. It was probably Rebecca, but if she didn't answer it her boss would think she'd taken an even longer lunch because of the stupid balloons. She picked up the phone. "Kat Young." It was Rebecca. She assured her she'd have the report on her desk by the end of the day. And she did.

§

...As the bus approached the Starbucks, Kat saw Marty's BMW parked in the corner of the lot, squeezed against the barrier so no one would ding his door. Exiting the bus, she felt a whirlwind of emotions. What could he have to say that was so important he couldn't say it on the phone? She crossed the lot to the coffee shop and entered, the rich smell of brewing coffee assaulting her senses. Marty was at a quiet table in the corner, sipping coffee, and there was a Starbucks cup in front of the empty chair opposite him. She pushed her way through the busy room to him. "I got you a vanilla latté," he said. "Is that OK?"

"It's OK, Marty," Kat said as she sat across from him. Why should she be impressed he remembered, when he'd seen her order it a hundred times? But she was. She pried the lid off and took a sip. "It's good, thanks."

"I'm glad you came," he said earnestly. "I don't know what I would have done if you hadn't."

Kat looked across the table at this man whom she'd tried to love. She'd never seen him like this, in such obvious pain, and so vulnerable. "It sounded urgent," she said. "No matter what befalls us, I could never turn my back if you were in need."

"It's more than that," Marty said. "I've been so anguished since the other night. Kat, I've been a jerk. I'm just so terribly, terribly sorry."

"I'll get over it," she said, a little sadly, more to her coffee cup than to anyone in particular. Behind her the barista pulled the lever on the espresso machine and the room filled with the gurgling and hissing of the steam jets.

"But that's just it," said Marty. *"I don't want you to get over it. Can you ever forgive me?"*

"The breakup was a shock, but maybe it's a good one; it's given me a chance to think about what I want in a relationship, what I need."

"Tell me what you need," said Marty desperately.

"What every woman needs: passion, romance, adventure," she said, looking him in the eye, unafraid.

"I want those things too, and I want them with you," he said, removing an aqua ring box from his pocket. He knelt beside her.

"Marty, what are you doing?" she said, suddenly aware that the buzz of conversation around them had stopped and the other customers were looking at them, smiling.

Marty opened the box to reveal a platinum engagement set with a sparkling flawless two-carat diamond.

"Kat, I've longed to say these words for the longest time. Is someone sitting here?" . . .

Kat looked up at the very pregnant woman indicating the seat currently occupied by her laptop case. "Sorry. Here, my stop's coming; I can get up." She picked up her computer and got to her feet. "So you won't have to let me out."

"Thank you," the woman said, collapsing into the seat with a great heaving sigh to let everyone around her know how over being pregnant she was.

Kat made her way to the front of the bus as they approached the corner in front of the Starbucks. Bending down, she saw Marty's BMW pull into the lot. She also saw the red pickup truck, parked at the opposite end of the lot, once again directly opposite the Starbucks' front door.

Kat stepped down to the curb. The lot was nearly full and Marty was parking in a space on the far corner of the lot, as close to the barrier as possible so his precious car wouldn't get dinged. She walked as quickly as she could to head him off, meeting him just as he got out of his car, which was directly in front of a small bakery, a funky sign in the window proclaiming "Caspian Corner." Kat saw there were two tables inside, by the window.

"Hi," he said tentatively, trying to gauge how angry she might be and wondering if she'd expect a hug. Marty had long since accepted he wasn't good at reading women's moods, so had decided it was better to always err on the side of caution.

"Hi," said Kat, very aware of the red truck and not wanting to have their meeting in Starbucks. "I'm not in the mood for corporate coffee today, let's try this place," she said, indicating the tiny bakery.

"Really?" he said, looking at the little bakery dubiously.

"Yeah, really. Come on, the whole world isn't Starbucks."

An old fashioned bell hanging on the door welcomed them as they entered the shop. Besides the tables, there were two glass display cases separated by a low counter with a cash register, where a pretty young Persian girl was talking on her phone. Behind her was a small, but professional-looking kitchen, with stainless counters and sink, a big Hobart mixer, Sub-Zero refrigerator and Wolf commercial stove and ovens. Kat sat at one of the tables by the window, with a clear view of the Starbucks.

"What do you want?" said Marty, studying the pastries in the display cases.

"A vanilla latté?" said Kat, her voice registering annoyance. *We're together eight years and he still has to effing ask?*

Marty walked over to the register as the girl said, "(She's such a slut!)" in Farsi into her phone. She turned her back on him and lowered her voice, more out of habit than real concern he could tell what she was saying; she'd never met an American who understood Persian. "(What did you do?)"

Ignored by the girl, Marty looked at the bear claws and doughnuts in the left display case. He looked back at Kat. "Want a doughnut?"

"No thanks."

Marty tapped on the display case, and the girl nodded, making the "just a minute" sign with her index finger as she scoffed into her phone, "(And she still did it? What a bitch!)" Marty tapped again, and the girl said, "(I've got to go, some stupid guy's here.)" She slapped the phone shut and looked at him, clearly annoyed. "What do you want?" she said, her American English perfect.

"Uh, black coffee and a latté." He pointed to a bear claw. "And one of those."

76

"That's eight-fifty-eight," she said, reading the amount on the register when she rang it up. Marty gave her a ten, and she dropped it in the drawer and pushed it shut. "There's cream and sugar," she said, nodding toward them on the display case as she poured his coffee in a Styrofoam cup. Then she slid open the display case, picked up a bear claw, appropriately enough with her bare hand, and dropped it on a paper plate.

"Uh, my change?" said Marty.

The girl opened the register and gave him a dollar and a quarter, then turned to make the latté. He briefly considered disputing the change discrepancy, then decided it wasn't worth it and took his coffee and bear claw to the table, muttering "What a lovely young woman," as he sat down.

Kat said, "So, you wanted to talk?"

Marty took a bite of his pastry, careful to avoid where the girl had touched.

"Uh, yeah, sorry about the other night."

"It was kind of a surprise."

"Your latté?" said the girl, her phone ringing. She began another conversation in Farsi as Marty fetched it and brought it back to the table.

"I didn't mean to hurt your feelings," he said, taking a sip of coffee. "Honestly, I'd never want to do that."

"I know," said Kat, thinking, *There's no point in fighting now.* She saw Cooper come out of the Starbucks carrying a cardboard cup. *Caffé Americano, black as night.* She tried her coffee, and nearly did a spit take. "My God!"

"What?" said Marty.

Kat looked at the girl, blabbing on her phone. "Excuse me!"

The girl turned her back to her, phone pressed to her ear. "(She said that? She's like the world's biggest liar!)"

Kat went to the counter. "Excuse me?"

"(Now this total bitch is here)," the girl said, her exasperation crossing the language barrier. "(I'll call you later.)" She slapped her phone shut and switched back to English. "What is it?"

Kat put her coffee on the counter. "There is something seriously wrong with this."

"It's just coffee and milk."

"Let me see the milk," said Kat.

The girl picked up the carton of milk from the counter beside the ovens and gave it to her.

"Are you crazy? It's, like, eighty in here. This belongs in the refrigerator."

"It usually is," said the girl, retreating a little now.

Kat read the expiration date. "And this should have been thrown out a week ago. If the health department saw this they'd shut you down on the spot."

"You can have your money back." The girl opened the register and gave her Marty's ten.

"Thank you," said Kat. She looked at the pastries in the left display case. "When did you bake these?"

"As if," sniffed the girl. "My dad buys them."

"How old are they?"

"I don't know, he throws the boxes away."

Kat looked at the other display case. "Are those Twinkies and Ho Hos?" she asked, incredulous.

She returned to Marty and slapped his ten on the table. "Come on." He took a last bite of the bear claw. "Isn't that thing stale?"

"A little," he said, washing it down with the last of his coffee. He stood up, pocketing the money, and followed her out to the parking lot.

"The world is losing its mind," she said.

"I don't know about the world," he said.

"What's that supposed to mean?"

"You're just so tense all the time," he said tentatively, sensing he was already on thin ice.

Kat realized at that moment she wanted nothing more than to punch him in the face.

"Look, I'm sorry, I didn't come here to fight," he said.

"What did you come here for then? Marty, I know I've given you a hard time about being indecisive, but I think we both need a little more time to think about this."

"Think about what?" he said.

"Uh, getting back together?"

"Oh, don't worry." He almost laughed with relief, realizing the misunderstanding, but a tiny voice inside his clueless boyhead told him this was a time for sincerity and seriousness. "That's not it. I wanted to make sure it's OK if I ask Tina out."

Kat reeled. He couldn't have actually said that. "Are you crazy?" she said, no longer bothering to keep the hysteria out of her voice.

"What's the problem? If you're OK with us breaking up…"

"Shut up, Marty," she said, cutting him off cold. "Know what? Go ahead. This will be fun to watch," she said as she stomped off, adding, "and fuck you very much for the poison birthday no-vanilla latté!"

§

Kat let herself into the dark house and pulled open the drapes, and soft evening light illuminated the shabby furniture and stained carpet. She sat on the sofa alone in the darkening room and put her face in her hands and sobbed.

Then there was a creaking sound, a door or soft footstep on oak floor and she looked up and listened. *Just the house cooling now the sun is gone.* She sat back and sighed a deep sigh, an emotional reset. Why Marty anyway? Because he'd been virtually unavailable? Well, no more virtual now, he *really* was. She heard the sound again, and a slight tingling chill ran up her back.

"Hello? Is someone there?" she said.

Silly. Still, should leave some lights on. Somebody might break in, although they'd be sorely disappointed, unless they were into music boxes and old half-empty perfume bottles. Her gaze fell on the ancient clock on the mantle. *Everything in this house needs a key.* She got to her feet and wound it, setting the time to the digital clock on her phone. Then she stood in the door to the kitchen and switched on the light. She leaned against the doorframe and closed her eyes, and the kitchen was spotless, the stove new, and everything bigger and better. Aunt Ruth, young and beautiful, removed a sheet of cookies from the oven, the smells mixing with her cologne. And her shoes, always so nice for every day.

Kat opened a door beneath the counter. Mixing bowls and muffin tins. A cupboard door revealed flour, sugar, baking powder, vanilla, cocoa and paper liners. She looked at the refrigerator. *Be afraid, be very afraid.* The butter hadn't reached its expiration date and the eggs were only a few weeks past it. *More of a guideline with eggs.* The milk was officially a biology experiment, but a return visit to the cupboard yielded a can of evaporated. She turned the oven to 375°.

Ninety minutes later Kat bent over a dozen cupcakes, already wearing a lemony silken glaze, expressing sugary roses on each with her aunt's pastry tube. Finished, she stood back and wiped her hands on her aunt's apron, admiring her work. Then her eyes fell on the drawer beneath the counter by the door. She opened it and saw the box of tiny birthday candles and the wooden matchbox. *A blue one.*

She place the candle squarely in the middle of the most perfect rose, then lit it, singing softly, "This is your birthday song and it's not very long…hey!" Then Kat closed her eyes, wishing with all her might, and blew it out. She was thirty years old.

five

Kat on a windswept ridge in the Santa Monica Mountains, a light breeze brushing hair across her face. Color fills the scene, so green, it must be spring. *Of course, wildflowers.* A man stands at the edge of the canyon, staring intently at something below. He doesn't hear her approaching. In fact there is no sound. She stands behind him and sees what fascinates, a pair of shiny black crows performing an aerial ballet in the updrafts. Turning and turning. Who knew birds could fly upside down? She wraps her arms around his chest and rests her head on his back, and feels his hands on hers.

The harsh bell of Kat's phone woke her rudely. *Got to change that damn alarm tone.* She let go of the pillow she'd held so tightly in her arms and lay back, arm over her eyes. Not nearly enough sleep, she'd got back to her apartment after two, in a cab. The bus was one thing, getting murdered was another. Cupcake scent drifted in from the kitchen, and she smiled. It had been as if Ruth had been looking over her shoulder. No way was she selling the house.

§

Kat stepped off the bus with her laptop, purse and a white cardboard pastry box, on time even, having sorted out the schedule. She bought a yogurt and banana on the short walk to the office, and arrived just as Tina turned the corner. Her friend was wearing a very un-Tina ensemble—a cropped blazer over slacks and heels.

"Look at you, job interview?" smiled Kat.

"Don't joke, Stuckie is breathing down my neck," said Tina. "And I don't have all your fuck-you money."

The glass doors parted and they entered the huge lobby together.

"What are you talking about?" Kat said as she stopped at Gus' station. She opened the box so he could choose a rose-crowned cupcake.

"Uh, the money from your aunt's house?" said Tina.

"Slight change of plan."

"You're not going to sell it?"

"I don't think so."

"It's a rat hole."

"You said you liked it."

"I was being supportive."

"Well, at least I don't have to worry about what to do with my nights and weekends for the next five years," Kat said as they proceeded to the elevators.

"Try ten," said Tina. "How was birthday at your mom's?"

Kat hesitated. "I have a confession to make. I didn't want to make it a big deal. I mean, I feel like this birthday is big enough, I'm officially middle-aged, for God's sake. I told my mother I was spending it with you guys."

"And you told us you were spending it with your mother. Nice."

"Sorry."

"No problem, we got drunk at lunch. So did you get lots of thinking done?"

"OK, one more confession. Marty called me and said he wanted to talk."

This stopped Tina in her tracks. "And?"

"I didn't know what he wanted, and know what? I didn't know what I wanted either, but I do now. He managed to convince me he's the world's biggest dick. The Marty chapter is definitely finis."

"I hope so," said Tina as they reached the elevators, "anyone who dreams about Prince Charming as much as you do doesn't deserve to end up with his evil half-brother Prince Whiny."

"Marty wasn't *that* bad," said Kat, quietly. Four more people had joined them, all staring at the digital numbers counting down. An elevator opened and everyone crowded on. As the doors were closing they heard Jason's voice. "Hold it!"

"Well, look who's here," Tina said under her breath, as someone held the doors for him.

"Can I fit?" he said a little out of breath, as everyone tried to make room.

"We can just squeeze you in," said the young woman holding the door, smiling a little too hard, in Kat's opinion.

"Morning, ladies," he said when he saw Kat and Tina. "I've got a conference call starting in, like, three minutes, and I called it. Bad form to be late for my own meeting." He eyed the pastry box. "Is someone celebrating today?"

"No way," said Tina, "she just makes these sick cookies and pastries."

"Really?" he said, seeming genuinely interested.

"I'll save you one," said Kat.

§

"I'll bet you will," said Tina when they'd stepped off on their floor and the doors had closed. "Speaking of Prince Charming."

"He's a colleague," said Kat as they walked the aisle of faceless cubicles.

"He's hot," said Tina as they reached Kat's space.

Kat sat down at her desk after putting the pastry box on the counter by her file cabinet. "Go ahead," she said. Tina opened it and gasped.

"Kind of a twelve-part birthday cake," said Kat.

"Beautiful," said Tina, making her selection. "Thanks, Marty."

"What do you mean?" said Kat.

"When bad shit happens to you, you bake."

"Thanks a lot."

"OK, that is a little selfish I guess," Tina said, taking a bite of her cupcake.

"Just a little," said Kat, logging on to her computer.

"Oh, Lord, what have we here?" Juanita was standing in the door.

"She saw Marty again last night, and it was cupcake bad," said Tina.

"Thank you Jesus," said Juanita, helping herself. "I thought you were going to your mom's," she said, taking her first succulent bite.

Another "What have we here?" was heard. It was John, a "temp" clerical who had been there over a year, blissfully young so he didn't need to worry about the health insurance or retirement the company wasn't providing him with.

"Cupcakes, have one," said Kat.

"You OK?" he said, helping himself to a rose-topped delight.

"I'm fine," said Kat, disgusted. "Just because I bake something doesn't mean my life's in crisis."

"Of course it doesn't," he said unconvincingly as he departed with his prize.

"I'm sorry I, you know, told you I was going to my mom's," Kat said to Juanita.

"Technically it was lying," said Tina.

"OK, whatever. Everything was happening at once, and then this stupid scary birthday. I just needed time to think."

"So, what you come up with?" said Juanita.

"She's not going to sell her aunt's house," said Tina.

"Good for you," said Juanita, finishing her cupcake. "Nice having a house, now you middle-aged."

"Juanita!" said Kat.

"I'm teasing you, honey. But it will be good. I'll bet it has an awesome kitchen, right?"

"It has a great kitchen. I mean, it's a little rough now…"

"Meaning it's filthy," said Tina.

"OK, but it will be worth cleaning up," said Kat.

"So, when do we start?" said Juanita.

"Seriously?" said Kat.

"And heavy lifting? My Boo's your man," said Juanita, eying the cupcakes again. "I'll just take one more for after lunch."

§

Kat put off calling the realtor as long as she could, but finally sucked it up and dialed her. Jacqueline was initially pissy and dismissive. Kat couldn't possibly be serious. I mean, she was never going to see an offer like that again. But when Kat convinced her she was very serious, adding that she wanted to restore it to its original condition, the woman immediately shifted gears, praising her decision, and promising her an even better price after the renovation. Kat, in turn, promised to keep her card, and tossed it as soon as she hung up. Then she ordered a dumpster, gave notice to her landlord (she'd already gone month-to-month because of the urine air freshener in the elevator and stairwell), and changed the utilities for her aunt's house into her name. This was the new take-charge, middle-aged Kat.

She pulled the lid off the yogurt and opened Outlook, scooping the creamy glop out with the convenience store plastic spoon as she scrolled through the email headers, efficiently prioritizing, her mind a precision instrument. Her phone rang, and reaching for it she spilled most of the yogurt on her keyboard. "Shit," she said, picking up the phone and wedging it between her ear and shoulder as she grabbed a handful of tissues. "Kat Young," she said as she sopped up as much yogurt as she could before it could reach the deadly electrical voltages she imagined lurking beneath the keys. It was a new district manager who started railing at her about a problem the woman had clearly caused in the first place. Kat calmly and efficiently explained this to her, at the same time praising her acumen for realizing the seriousness of the situation before it got out of hand, effectively handing her a lovely shit sandwich.

As she hung up, she felt a PRESENCE in her doorway and swiveled her chair around. It was Max, tapping his messenger bag against his knee in the unconscious manner a cat twitches its tail. He didn't seem more uncomfortable than normal. Did this mean the techie she'd spoken to after she'd seen his stalker gallery had told the truth when he said he wouldn't tell him she'd been there? Also, there had been several shots of her at her desk. Had he just taken another? He had his other hand in his pocket. Was that a spy camera or was he just glad to see her? "What is it, Max?" she said, deciding to postpone their come-to-Jesus conversation about the pictures for a time when she didn't have eighteen things on her mind.

"Updates," he said defensively.

"Oh, God, not now. It's Friday. Every minute I spend watching you screw with my computer is another minute I'll spend working on my weekend."

"It's not 'screwing with' your computer, they're security-dictated. A single unprotected machine could bring down the entire company and everybody else on the floor is done."

"How long will it take?" she sighed, recognizing a losing battle.

"Not long."

Kat stood up, crossed her arms and leaned against the doorframe. He sat down, opened his bag and took out a hand-labeled CD-ROM.

"Have you had those socks since high school?" she asked as he inserted the disc in the drive tray.

"My socks are no concern of yours," said Max precisely. He started to type in his password, but immediately lifted his fingers from the keys. "This is all sticky. What's on here?"

"I have one of those really phlegmy colds?"

"That is so not funny," he said as he whipped open his bag, where a brief frantic search produced a small bottle of hand sanitizer. He liberally squirted his hands, then grabbed a handful of tissues from the box on her desk.

"Help yourself."

When he'd dried his hands and deposited the tissues neatly in the wastebasket, he opened the disc drive on her computer, returned his CD to its envelope and dropped it into his bag.

"What are you doing?" asked Kat.

"You've ruined your keyboard," he said matter-of-factly. "I'll have to get you another one before I can do you."

"Max, if we live a thousand years, you will never 'do' me," she said, instantly regretting the joke.

"Ha ha," he said as he got to his feet and went to the doorway. "Wait till your next total crash, when you're in the middle of one of your hysterical meltdowns. Then it'll be 'Oh, please Max, can you drop everything you're doing and fix this now?'"

"OK, you're right. I'm sorry," Kat said, marveling that she was somehow the one being made to feel bad. She started to sit down, then noticed he was still there, his back to her. When he turned back around his mouth was tight, his face beet red.

"Shin told me you saw the, you know…"

So they *were* going to talk about it now. "Uh, yeah," said Kat. "It felt kind of strange."

"I took them down," he said.

"Probably a good idea."

"I only did it because I think you're nice," he blurted, then spun around and disappeared up the aisle.

Kat looked at the empty doorway for a moment, then sat down. *Perfect, now I feel guilty for hurting my stalker's feelings.*

She touched the keyboard. It *was* pretty gross.

§

That night she fixed herself some light pasta. As she washed it down with a Trader Joe's four-dollar

91

Viognier she looked at her furniture and considered the terror of moving. Her eyes fell on the book boxes. One advantage to not having unpacked them when she moved in was not having to pack them to move out. But now there would be shelves aplenty, and she wouldn't be moving again for a long time. Maybe never. Her aunt didn't.

six

Tina picked Kat up just after nine Saturday morning, and a truer sign of friendship there never was, given she hadn't gotten home from the clubs until three AM. She was dressed for serious cleaning in sequined flip-flops, extreme cut-offs that revealed a fourth of her butt cheeks, and a tight pink T-shirt that read, "GO AWAY!" in front and, "(Come back!)" behind.

"Boo's helping us; Juanita's going to hate those pants," said Kat.

"Juanita needs to get over herself, and they're not pants, they're shorts," said Tina.

"No kidding," said Kat, as Tina leaned into the VW loading boxes, revealing a generous amount of darling cheek.

They stopped at the Starbucks to fuel up and Tina noticed Kat glance at the parking lot several times while they were waiting to order. "Expecting someone?" she asked.

"Just checking out my new neighborhood," Kat lied, torn between wanting to see the red truck and not wanting to see the red truck.

When Tina parked in front of the house they sat quietly for a moment looking at it, until she said, "I didn't notice the stained glass in the door before."

Kat said, "It's a Craftsman thing, and the way the eves extend all around the house."

"It really is cool. Is that a fruit tree?"

"I'm pretty sure it's a lemon. I remember Ruth making the best fresh lemonade. My mother got mad when I told her about it, probably because we always had Kool-Aid made with too much water, so the packages would go farther."

As they got out of the car the truck arrived with the rollaway dumpster, the driver so distracted by Tina's shorts he nearly took out the neighbor's fence as he parked the steel container in Kat's driveway.

They decided to start with the living room carpet, but there was the problem of the furniture. The sofa and chairs were ragged, stained and smelly, the coffee and side tables delaminating and blistered. A floor lamp was missing its glass bowl and the finish was worn off. But still...

"I planned on throwing most of it away," said Kat. "That's why I got the dumpster. But now I feel weird about it."

"You have nice furniture," said Tina. "And your aunt wanted you to have the house. That means it's yours now."

They got the chairs and the tables out and into the dumpster, but couldn't get the sofa through the door, even when Tina took off her sandals. They were studying the problem when Juanita and Boo parked their mini-van behind the roll-away in the driveway. Juanita lowered the passenger window and barked at them. "Hold on there, somebody gonna' break a nail."

The pair exited the van and Juanita, holding a plastic bucket full of cleaning supplies, stood on the sidewalk checking out the house. Boo, dressed for success with a thick gold chain around his neck, Laker's polo shirt, shiny calf-length basketball shorts, calf-length white socks and high-top sneakers, walked across the lawn, saying "Yo, ladies, get away from that!" He picked up the sofa like it was a huge loaf of bread and lifted it through the front door.

"I do love a big strong man," said Juanita.

"Where you want this thing?" said Boo, not even breaking a sweat.

"In the dumpster?" said Kat, wondering how he was going to manage it.

"No way, this clean up nice," he said.

"You're welcome to have it," said Kat.

"Put it in the box," Juanita said firmly.

"But…" Boo tried.

"No buts, we got a garage full of stuff now 'clean up nice' that never seem to get cleaned up," said Juanita, ending the conversation.

"Where are the kids?" Kat asked her, as Boo lifted the sofa over his head and lowered it gently into the steel box.

"With their nana," said Juanita.

"It's so sweet of you guys to help me out," said Kat.

"Honey, any day they're with his mother is a vacation," said Juanita. "And when they come back from Nana's? They mind. She run kiddy boot camp."

"That's the Lord's truth," said Boo. "First day of basic that drill sergeant had nothin' on my mama."

Juanita stepped into the house, rubbing her hands together. "Now what kind of trouble we got here?"

Tina was on all fours, her back to the door, as she pulled up the far corner of the carpet, and Juanita did a double take at her shorts.

"Girl, where the rest of your pants?"

"Juanita?" Tina said carefully without looking at her. "It's Saturday."

"I think they look nice," said Boo, entering behind her.

"You ain't here to think," said Juanita evenly.

Tina stepped back while Boo tore the edges of the carpet up. He had it rolled and in the dumpster in less than five minutes. The hallway, bedroom and study carpeting followed, along with the mattress from Ruth's bed. Kat was definitely keeping the bed, however (in fact, she'd already ordered a new mattress), as well as the vanity, bench and chest of drawers. She'd have them refinished someday, or not. She kind of liked their shabby chic patina. Of course, the roll-top desk in the guest bedroom-turned study had to stay, as well as its chair, a locked steamer trunk, and the bookshelves that covered every wall of the room. She'd sort through the books later.

The verdict on the hardwood floors was they just wanted a good cleaning and polish. Boo rented a polisher, while Juanita attacked the kitchen and bathroom tile with her magical cleaning powers. By the end of the day the kitchen and bath shone, if not like new, at least like clean, and didn't even "stink" (per Tina). The floors were almost lustrous and the keeper furniture was back in place. It felt like a home. A really pretty home.

The four did a walk through, ending in the study, and their eyes fell on the steamer trunk.

"You want me to get that open?" said Boo. "I could probably pop that old thing with screwdriver," referring to the locked hasp.

"No," said Kat, "I don't want to break it. The key must be around here someplace."

Tina made a run for cashew chicken, seared tuna salads and spicy dumplings. The rusty dinette and chairs had joined the carpeting in the dumpster, so they spread a blanket on the living room floor and sat around a red wine bottle candle holder like picnickers (the red wine poured into plastic cups) and ate and drank, and Kat's first toast in her new house was to her best friends forever.

§

That night in her apartment Kat was jumping out of her skin with anticipation. She crashed early, but couldn't sleep, so she made a pot of coffee and started packing.

She was back at the house first thing Sunday morning, stocking the refrigerator and cupboards with the basics. She wished the mattress she'd ordered was already there so she could spend the night, but it wouldn't be delivered until Tuesday. She would schedule the movers Monday, but there was still so much to do she decided she'd have to take a couple of vacation days. That settled, she de-stressed the best way she knew, and soon there was a shiny sheet of steel on the counter with a batch of plump peanut butter cookies, the house filled with their rich scent.

Her primal need to bake satisfied, she started sorting through Ruth's books. Their libraries couldn't have been more different. Ruth's was based in the classic novels of the Nineteenth Century and thick with wonderful Twentieth-century novelists and travel and adventure. Kat's was fluffy by comparison, Romance novels and popular fiction, books bought at airport bookstores and raced through before destination city and work could end the escape. But escape was what they shared, the chance to live inside another's consciousness, and most specifically for Kat, to escape her own. She'd put out a large box for books she planned to donate, but after an hour there were only three in it. Then she found Beryl Markham's *West With The Night* and settled back against the wall, her knees to her chest, and journeyed to colonial Kenya.

Two hours later Kat's rumbling stomach reminded her it was almost noon and she put Markham aside. She briefly considered the cookies, but stowed them safely away in a pastry box, deciding to walk up to Olympic and see what was open. Navigating the sidewalk, the Jacaranda was like a purple cloud ceiling pierced by brilliant mid-day sun, her neighbor's lawns like the veldt stretching to the horizon.

...The engine ran rough: ta-pocketa-ta-pocketa-cough, and Kat adjusted the fuel mixture on the little silver ship till it purred pocketa-pocketa again, the aircraft rocking in the updrafts high above the plains of Kenya. She was headed up-country to pick up a gaggle of big game hunters and normally would be anticipating the job with bored resignation, but it would be good to get out of Nairobi for a few days to clear her head. When Jason Stevens had arrived from London and word spread about the handsome, wealthy bachelor, Kat had

been safely and comfortably engaged, albeit to a man who was perpetually (and safely) unavailable. So when Stevens had approached her about developing an East African air passenger service, she had been thrilled to realize her long-time dream. But there had been something else there from their first meetings, he in his Savile Row suits, with their faint air of verbena and cedar and she in the khaki mufti she'd worn since adopting this wild country as her home, something troubling that aroused the womanhood she'd so successfully stifled and sublimated. And he must have sensed it too, because when he learned her engagement was ended he had taken her in his strong arms and kissed her as she'd never been kissed. And, truth be told, she'd returned his kiss with equal fervor, in spite of her longstanding rule about mixing business with her personal life. Yes, it would be good to have some time to herself to sort things out.

She dipped the port wing, the controls light in her hands, till a small way station airport appeared in the distance, and she saw a familiar red transport parked in front of the lonely hanger. She checked her fuel gauge. She would have to refuel at some point on the journey, but could wait for the return leg. Then she chided herself, she'd made a mistake when her wing had clipped the tail of his aircraft on the tarmac in Nairobi, but *every pilot makes mistakes, and there had been a stiff crosswind on the runway...*

Cooper was just getting out of his truck, characteristically parked directly in front of the Starbucks, as Kat walked onto the parking lot. "Wouldn't it be easier to just hook up a caffeine drip?" she smiled.

"Not a bad idea," he said, seemingly unsurprised to see her.

"I don't seem to be getting anywhere with fixing your truck, how about I buy you a latté?"

"Am I allowed a black coffee?" he said.

"Oh, yes, I remember now, caffé Americano, black as night."

"She's a very dramatic barista, evidently working on a screenplay," he said, pushing the door of his truck closed.

"I think they all are," said Kat, glancing at the little bakery in the corner of the strip mall as she followed him into the shop. Caspian Corner was deserted, as usual.

There was one person ordering as they queued up. "Anyway, black coffee isn't a problem," said Kat. "In fact, anything on the menu. Go nuts. I just got paid."

Cooper looked at her curiously. "So, you said you just moved here?"

"Not to LA, just the neighborhood. My aunt left me her house."

"Nice aunt."

"Really nice aunt," said Kat. "It's a lovely old Craftsman, a little long of tooth, but good bones."

"Interesting, I have one too, a 1913 bungalow I saved from being torn down to make way for a five-thousand-square-foot monster," he said. "Does it need a lot of work? Mine's a never-ending saga."

"I'm sure there's lots I could do to it, but for now I'm just happy at how nice it looks cleaned up a bit."

"I'd like to see it sometime," said Cooper, as the customer in front of them finished.

"How about now?" said Kat, surprising herself with her courage.

"Cool," said Cooper, and it was.

"Next?" said the Starbucks cashier.

Cooper looked at Kat. "What do you want?"

"A vanilla latté."

"And Caffé Americano for me," Cooper told the barista, then looked at the display of pastries and sandwiches. "Anything I want, right?" he said to Kat.

"Anything your heart desires."

He indicated a row of cookies to the girl behind the counter. "Are those peanut butter?"

"On second thought, hold off on the cookies," said Kat.

§

Kat clambered into the red truck that had survived her kamikaze attack. It had been painstakingly restored, but still had a great old truck smell and feel and made amazing noises when Cooper put it into gear and released the clutch. "Take a right," said Kat, "it's the next to the last house on the block on the right."

Cooper steered his truck onto the street. "I love the Jacaranda this time of year, they're like purple clouds," he said.

"I was just imagining flying through them," said Kat. "Do you really need Starbucks for black coffee?"

"I work at home. It's good to be among other humans a few times a day," he said. "It keeps me from going feral."

"What do you do?"

"I'm an artist."

"You make a living at it?" wondered Kat.

"Depends on your definition of living," he smiled.

"This is it," said Kat, pointing to her little house. "You can park in the driveway behind the dumpster."

Cooper pulled in, switched off the engine and stepped on the floor-peddle emergency brake, which made a safe mechanical sound. "What a great little house," he said.

"The yard's kind of a mess," said Kat.

"That's the easiest part," said Cooper. "That's an amazing stained glass tree on the door. Like a smaller version of the one at the Gamble house."

"It is a tree, isn't it?" Kat said, a little surprised. "It gives the room a wonderful green glow when the sun hits it in the morning."

"You just noticed it's a tree?"

"More like remembered. There's something peculiar about this house for me. At first it was hard for me to see it, but everyday it gets easier, like it's coming into focus."

§

"Almost none of my stuff is here yet," said Kat as she let them in the front door, "just a few boxes of books and some kitchen stuff. I'm going to try to move in this week."

"You leave your windows open?" said Cooper.

"I'm trying to air it out a little."

"I think it's an OK neighborhood, but you should still probably lock up when you leave."

"Advice taken, officer."

"Awesome," said Cooper, admiring the floor. "It isn't refinished, right?"

"It was carpeted. All I did was pull it up and polish it. I mean, my friends helped."

He ran his hand along the redwood mantle over the fireplace. "I've been working on stuff in my place for five years, and it isn't this nice yet."

He looked in the kitchen. "What a great old stove. The one in my place was gone when I bought it." He ran his hand over the gleaming porcelain and chrome. "I thought about finding one of these, but I'm pretty serious about food and went with a new Wolf."

"Stainless steel?" Kat asked. *What a stupid question.*

"Black enamel, actually. I liked the way it looked with the red dog on the oven door," he said, taking the lid off his coffee.

"Speaking of serious food," said Kat, picking up the pastry box, "here's why I suggested holding off on the Starbucks cookies." She held the lid open while he chose one. She watched as he took a bite.

"I just had a religious experience," he said. "These can't be from around here, I have every good bakery scoped."

"They came from that little oven," she said, indicating the O'Keefe & Merritt.

He gobbled the rest of it, speaking with his mouth full. "Did you use some kind of amazing frozen dough?"

"Do you paint by numbers?" said Kat.

"From scratch? My abject apologies." He looked wistfully at the box. "Please ma'am, may I have another?" She opened the box for him and he chose the fattest of the lot.

"Good choice," said Kat. She put the box down and peeled the lid off her coffee as Cooper wandered back into the living room. She started to follow him, then looked at the pastry box. *Cookies for lunch after all.*

Cooper asked if he could see the rest of the house. He pronounced the bathroom in amazing condition and loved the tile and stained glass, saying it looked like an unrenovated-looking renovation. He agreed Ruth's bedroom set was perfect for the room, and was fascinated by her study, especially the mysterious steamer trunk.

"These were your aunt's?" he said, surveying the titles on the bookshelves.

"Yes," said Kat, "the boxes are mine. I'm trying to decide what to keep. It's hard."

"No kidding, she had great taste. I have this one," he said, selecting a well-thumbed copy of Flaubert's *L'Éducation sentimentale.* "A Sentimental Education, a French edition, no less. Have you read it?"

"No," said Kat, "and I won't be starting with the French version."

"My copy's a translation. It's wonderful, the most perfect book about friendship I've ever read."

He knelt beside one of the boxes on the floor and looked at the titles curiously. "Are these all…"

"Romance?" said Kat, feeling sillier by the minute and hoping he didn't say something about bodice rippers.

"I was going to say bodice rippers."
Perfect.
He selected one. "The Blue-Eyed Witch."

"Barbara Cartland's actually a pretty good writer," Kat said defensively. "I mean, maybe not Flaubert…in French." *Now he thinks I'm an idiot.*

"I'm sure she's been translated," he smiled. He turned it over to read the back cover blurb out loud. "This Raven-haired blue-eyed beauty was casting a spell on him, bewitching him as no other woman had done before." He looked up at Kat. "Sounds like this guy's in serious trouble." He put it back in the box and scanned the rest of the titles. "You must have everything she ever wrote."

"Not even close, that would be, like, six or seven hundred books."

Cooper returned his attention to Ruth's collection, putting his finger on a volume of Cormac Macarthy's Border Trilogy. "Have you read *All The Pretty Horses*? It's probably the most romantic book I've ever read."

"No," said Kat. "There was a movie, right?"

"Yeah, did you like it?"

"Didn't see it," said Kat, confident if she hadn't already cinched her idiot status with Cooper, that did it.

"It was the pale shadow of the book," he said absently as he selected an antique-looking copy of Cinderella, the original Perrault version, with its Doré cover illustration.

"OK, I've read that one," she said. "Cinderella is every little girl's first romance novel, at least where the heroine is awake for most of the story."

Cooper opened it to a fabulous illustration of Cinderella surrounded by noblemen, as the prince fits the fateful pump onto her dainty foot.

"Then we realize there aren't actually any princes or glass slippers," she added.

"That's so sad," said Cooper.

"It is," Kat laughed, "especially after you spend your entire time growing up planning on the moment when he shows up and slips it onto your foot."

Cooper shelved the book and straightened up. "I'd better get going. I'm preparing for a show and I'll be up all night as it is."

"A show of your work?"

"Yeah. If you're interested, I'll stick an invite in your mailbox."

"I'd love that," said Kat, following him out of the room, but Cooper stopped her in the hall entry to the living room.

"Wait," he said quietly. "You have an intruder."

"Oh my God."

"It's OK, not the kind I was warning you about, but he probably did come in through the open window."

She followed his gaze to a dove perched on the mantle, which took wing when it saw them, circling the room twice before it settled back down above the fireplace.

"Open the door," Cooper said, "it might follow the light out."

Kat went to the door, the movement freaking the bird, which frantically circled the room again, this time lighting on a sconce. Cooper moved toward it, arms out, and the bird did another circuit of the room, returning to the sconce.

"Should we call somebody?" Kat had never had a bird in her house before.

But Cooper put his hands together and blew in a hole between his thumbs, making a cooing sound. The bird cocked its head, evidently impressed that he spoke dove, and flew straightaway to his shoulder. Cooper walked slowly to the door and out onto the porch. Man and bird enjoyed a moment, then the bird took wing, disappearing through the Jacaranda cloud.

"Wow, I can't believe that just happened," said Kat, coming to the door.

"It must be somebody's bird, you know, trained to do that," he said.

"How did you know?"

"I didn't," he said, "it just seemed like a good idea at the time." He looked at her thoughtfully. "This was nice. Maybe we can do this again after my, uh… "

"Show?"

"Right, my show."

"Wait," said Kat as she hurried back to the kitchen. She picked up the pastry box and brought it back to the front door. "Take these, for that sugar rush when you start to run down tonight."

"I couldn't take your whole box."

"Please, I was just going to take them to work tomorrow, and my co-workers are fat and spoiled. Call it a contribution to the arts."

"Awesome," he said taking it. "This was nice. Like I started to say, maybe we can do it again. I mean, are you seeing anyone?"

Kat laughed, surprised by this.

"Sorry, I…"

"It's OK," she interrupted, "it's nice to feel noticed. I actually just got out of an eight year relationship and I'm not sure I'm ready for the deep end of the dating pool quite yet." Kat had always been a one-thing-at-a-time kind of person when it came to men and, while she technically hadn't started "seeing" Jason (well, outside work and her industrial-strength imagination), he was the closest thing to a real live prince she'd ever encountered, and she was intrigued by the possibilities.

He stepped down from the porch. "Well, I'll just crawl back into my cave."

"Your sad, dark, dank, lonely cave," said Kat.

"Exactly," he said.

"Tell you what: how about I bring my girlfriend to your show? She's adorable. Asian. Turns men into Jell-O."

"That will be very thoughtful of you. So, see you 'round the neighborhood. Like I said, it was nice." He walked to his truck, and Kat closed the door, more than a little amazed.

seven

...Strolling on the Champs-Élysées after gorging themselves at Guy Savoy on artichoke with black truffle soup and fat lobsters, washed down with the richest white burgundy (and ending with espresso and perfect mille-feuille), Jason held her hand in public for the first time. Even though she accepted that because of their high-level positions in the company they had to leave Los Angeles, traveling all the way to Paris for such a gesture to be safe, it still made her heart ache, because she wanted so much for them to be able to live and celebrate their love openly. The streetlamps glistened on the cobblestones, wet from the light rain, and her heart sang, feeling his strong hand in hers. They had been in Paris two days, barely leaving their tiny, elegant hotel, making love with a desperation born of the knowledge they must

111

soon return to the lie they lived every day in California.
She had never felt so free, and yet a happy slave to this
*man…*who appeared to be wrapping up his
presentation.

Jason leaned over the end of the table, balancing
on his fingertips, and spoke to Rebecca and her staff
with the intensity and earnestness of a true believer: "In
chapter three, *Attack by Stratagem*, of Sun Tzu's The Art
Of War, he discusses the power of unity in planning
and attack. In an ever more complex economic
environment it's vital that departments work, and grow
together. This project will be an ideal proving ground
for us as a corporation, setting the stage for potential
dominance in the twenty-first century."

Kat smiled at this, translating it in her mind. *I'll*
need your best people, and all your projects will be on hold until
it's completed, at which time they may be promoted into my
division. Without looking she knew Rebecca, sitting
beside her, was jumping out of her skin.

"I'm sure you have questions," said Jason as he
closed his PowerPoint presentation.

"I'm not seeing new here," said Rebecca. "We've
tried similar rollouts two or three times since I've been
with the company."

Meaning since the Clinton administration, thought Kat.
The meeting was into its third hour. Tina, sitting across
from her, had the desperate glazed look of a feral cat

trapped in an Animal Services cage. Someone's stomach rumbled.

...Paris sparkled in the moonlight as the elevator carried them ever higher above the starry city lights. Kat knew something was afoot; Jason had been oddly secretive and excited the entire evening, even more attentive and doting than usual. And now, sharing a kiss that promised to last the length of the ride to the most romantic view in the world, Kat knew in her heart that dreams were for coming true. When the doors opened and their lips reluctantly parted, they stepped from the lift onto the windswept platform high above the city, and Kat's heart soared. In that moment she knew that a selfless union of spirit and minds could accomplish any goal. She stepped to the dizzyingly high railing and looked down on the tiny people and cars moving below them, noticing, oddly, an old red American pickup truck among the Peugeots, Citroens, BMWs and Mercedes. Then she felt him close behind her, the faintest scent of verbena and cedar. He opened his cashmere topcoat and wrapped it and his arms around her, then pressed his lips to her ear. "You've barely spoken, Kat. How do you feel about this?"...

Kat blinked at him, aware that Rebecca especially was waiting for her answer. "I, uh…" Tina was looking at her, but the six other people at the meeting besides

113

Rebecca, Tina, Jason and herself were probably thinking about lunch. "I think the selfless union of spirit and minds can accomplish any goal."

Jason was momentarily taken aback, but recovered quickly. "Wow," he said, "that's exactly...I mean, you nailed it. That's what this project is about, creating new business models and the future of MartCo. I'm really pleased to hear you say that."

Yeah, well, Kat knew Rebecca wasn't. She decided to wait till after lunch to tell her boss she needed to take a couple of vacation days for her move.

§

Kat got a stale tuna sandwich and a Coke from the machines and spent lunch at her desk, pounding it in a futile effort to make up for the lost morning. She was so behind even before the meeting she would normally have had to work half the night, but she would have to pack—the movers were booked. Further bad news, she'd scored some boxes from the Ralph's, but had already exhausted her supply. She'd have to somehow get to U-Haul. She was rethinking the whole no car thing when Tina came back from lunch. She picked up the cellophane wrapper from Kat's sandwich.

"Was this that tuna that's been in the machine since last Thursday?" she said, grimacing.

"OK, yeah, I ate at my desk. I have to get this done by five because I have to somehow figure out how to get to U-Haul to pick up more boxes because I haven't finished packing and..."

"No problem," interrupted Tina, "I'll drive you. I can help you pack too if you want, but you have to feed me."

"God, Teen, you're a lifesaver," said Kat. "That meeting put me so behind, and can you believe what I said to Jason?"

"What did you say?" asked Tina, totally serious.

"You were there. I mean, it looked like you were there."

"I know. Cool, huh?" she said as she returned to her cubicle.

§

At precisely five PM, her purse and laptop over her shoulder and a folder in hand, Kat knocked lightly on her boss's door, which was slightly ajar. Rebecca was on the phone and gave her the one minute finger in the air, but indicated for her to sit. Kat had decided not to take Tina's advice about just calling in sick for the move, but sitting across from Rebecca now she started to get cold feet. Rebecca rang off on her call and spoke to Kat in the same breath. "Do you have my numbers?"

"All here," Kat said, handing her the folio. "There are two regional managers who are way off. I'll have to work with them."

"Work with them?" said Rebecca flipping through the pages. "What about just replacing them? We could probably save ten-thousand a year on their salaries."

Kat remembered Tina speculating that Rebecca might have a red hourglass birthmark on her abdomen. She said, "Beyond the fact that there may be other factors, what kind of message does that send to our other people?"

"A damn good message," said Rebecca. "A message that in this economy nobody gets a free ride."

Kat decided to call in sick. "You may be right. Let me talk to them; see what's really going on with the territories."

"They're your team members, you're ultimately responsible, but it's your call," said Rebecca. "Are you leaving? You're usually the last one here."

"I'm…not feeling very well," said Kat, shifting gears in mid-sentence as she got to her feet. "It might have been the tuna sandwich I got from the machine today, so I could eat lunch at my desk?"

"We need to change vendors for those machines," said Rebecca, looking for something in her desk drawer. "I had some egg salad last week that was growing fur."

Kat had almost reached the door when Rebecca stopped her. "Kat, can I talk you about something else for one minute?"

"Sure," Kat said, wishing she'd made it out.

"Be careful with Jason Stevens."

You could have pushed Kat over with a feather. "What do you mean?" she said, as calmly as possible.

"You're an exemplary employee. Your reviews have all been nearly perfect, and not just the ones you've seen. The confidential reviews I've written for you for Mr. Martin have emphasized how careful and thoughtful and complete your work has been, and what an asset you are."

To say this wasn't what Kat expected to hear would be understatement of historic proportions. Rebecca leaned back in her chair, adopting a positively sisterly tone. "If you wanted to work in Jason's division I'd miss you, but I wouldn't hold you back from an opportunity. But Jason is definitely looking out for Jason, and certain people are aware of that. He might not be the best place to be hitching your star, as it were."

"Well…that's certainly something to think about, and I'm glad you're happy with my work. Like I said, I don't feel so good," Kat said, desperate to be out of there.

"Go on, take care of yourself. We can discuss this more later, if you want," said Rebecca.

Man, did Kat ever not want to discuss it more later. "OK, I'll see you tomorrow," she lied, edging out the door.

§

Tina needed to change and take her grandmother to the grocery store, but promised to pick up some boxes and meet Kat at her apartment. The bus was full enough that people were standing, but Kat found a seat, and the guy she sat down beside, with what appeared to be a full grocery bag in his lap, wasn't even smelly. The conversation with Rebecca had thrown her. Rebecca had been her boss for almost five years and in that time she'd been consistently demanding, difficult and distant. Kat didn't know what to make of this apparent reversal. It was gratifying to hear that Rebecca appreciated her work and had voiced her appreciation to the head of the company, but Kat didn't understand her criticism of Jason, especially after witnessing Rebecca acting like a giddy schoolgirl whenever he spoke to her. *I mean, it's one thing to fantasize. Harmless, really.* Kat didn't seriously think that Jason might be the one, but it was fun to think of him, of being with him in that way, how solid and confidant he was, how safe it would feel to be in his arms and how thrilling his kiss.

...the flight attendant waiting at the top of the Gulf V's fold-down stairway smiled as Kat and Jason climbed the stairs. "Welcome back, Ms. Young, Mr. Stevens." She stowed their roll-away bags as they made their way to the deep leather seats.

"I'm glad you were able to reschedule so you could help me out with this," said Jason, loud enough for the flight attendant to hear. The company's strict anti-fraternization policy for its executives made it imperative that no one suspect that along with the flurry of whirlwind, game-changing meetings the two would be directing, they would also be very secretly engaged in mind-bending, passionate love-making.

"I'm glad I was able to," said Kat, slightly dizzy from the faint scent of verbena and cedar she sensed when he took off his coat, and pushing the thought of their last kiss from her mind, the deepest, hottest kiss two lovers had shared in the history of the world.

As Jason slid into the seat beside her, he leaned in and whispered "Take a look at this..."

"What?" said Kat, surprised her bus seatmate had spoken so closely to her ear.

"Take a look at this," the guy repeated with a weird smile. He moved the grocery bag just enough to reveal that by "this" he meant his erect penis, which had a purple tinge, probably because he'd been squeezing it.

119

"Hmm," said Kat thoughtfully, and stood up, gathering her purse and laptop. She pushed her way to the front, where she gripped the chrome pole and leaned over the driver as the bus lurched down Olympic Boulevard. "This guy back there showed me his penis."

"Are you sure?" said the driver as he accelerated to get through an intersection before the light changed.

§

Tina's jaw dropped. "That's all he said?"

"He was right, it might have been, you know, some kind of growth or one of those hairless cats, or even a Japanese eggplant," Kat said, slurping Chinese noodles from a cardboard take out container. "But I'm still pretty sure it was a purple penis. I've been rethinking the whole no car thing anyway. The house is a lot farther from work, and I have to transfer."

"I couldn't do the bus in LA," said Tina. "But, you know, I don't crash into things."

"I can drive," said Kat. "I just need to focus. I think this last accident is going to make a major difference. I just need to focus," she repeated, more for her benefit than for Tina's.

"You mean be on the same astral plain as everybody else?"

"Thank you, Marty," sniffed Kat. "Anyway, wasn't I supposed to be feeding you?"

"You just sounded so distraught on the phone," said Tina as she picked up a potsticker with her splintery chopsticks. "And I was in Asia Town with my gram anyway and this place is right in the market."

"This is great," said Kat, laying smoked tofu on a thin pancake and slathering it with plum sauce. "Your grandma sounds funny."

"It totally freaked her out when I told her I'm helping you move into a house where somebody just died. Old Thai people are, like, obsessed with ghosts."

"Even if you do believe in that stuff, my aunt was a nice lady."

"It doesn't matter. If someone you know has a bad death they can return and sit on your head or your back, making you bend over. They call that one *Phi Pawb*."

"That *one*?" said Kat, washing down her pancake with a swig of tangy Chinese beer.

"There's dozens of different kinds. Actually, it could be hundreds. That's why a lot of Thais, Chinese people too, only buy new houses. They're afraid they'll wake up and there'll be a bloody head floating in the air beside the bed, looking at them."

"Well, it would actually be kind of cool to see my aunt again. Not just her head, of course."

"Don't even say that," said Tina, wide eyed.

"I thought you said only old Thai people believe in that stuff."

"I didn't say that. You should offer her something after you're moved in. Something she liked to eat or drink."

"Like what?" said Kat.

"What did she like?"

"God, I think she ate just about anything. She was an amazing cook. Her pastries were out of this world."

"Maybe that's where you get it."

"Maybe. And she liked martinis. She'd make a pitcher of them and have me pour for her while she was reading a book to me or while we were baking."

"There you go—leave her some pastries and a martini. The main thing is you want her to be happy. The last thing you want in your house is an unhappy ghost. They can get ugly. There's this one my gram told me about when I was a little girl, Phi Kra-sue, that looks like a really pretty lady who floats along in this long flowing dress, but underneath it there's just her organs and intestines flapping around like the legs of a squid or something and she can fly at you and attach her mouth to your face or neck."

"How old were you when she told you this?" asked Kat.

"I don't know, three or four. I had nightmares"

"Did your mother know she was telling you this stuff?"

"Gram told her the same shit when she was growing up."

Ghostly suggestion? Kat would wonder about this later.

§

In T-shirt and panties, her bare foot braced on her knee like a Masai herdsman, Kat brushed her teeth, while running her fingers over the tile on the wall behind the pedestal sink. The move had gone like clockwork (after calling in sick to work, of course). Her furniture blended nicely with those pieces of Ruth's she'd decided to keep. When the new mattress was delivered she thought, *There it is: my credit card is officially full.* A car passed in the street and the stained glass window glowed green and red and orange. She'd removed the curtains, rod and bracket; the colored glass provided plenty of privacy. She'd need to fill the screw holes and paint the molding. Another weekend project. She spit toothpaste foam, then took a slug of mouthwash from the bottle and spit again, carefully rinsing the sink.

It would take many weekends before there was a place for everything and everything was in its place, but the kitchen and bathrooms were sorted out, and her clothes were mostly hung, folded and put away. Well, mostly. Moving was an ideal time to edit one's wardrobe, so there were a few piles here and there in the bedroom, but her new old bed was made and her bottles and things were arranged neatly on the vanity, and the music box had migrated to the dresser.

She stopped in the bathroom doorway to her bedroom. The lamp on the nightstand now had a white hundred-watt bulb for reading and an amber twenty-five for mood. The latter was on, and it gave the space a fairy tale feeling, softly illuminating the bed's warm dark wood and the heavily beveled mirror of the vanity. Kat sighed and slid under the sheets, feeling a vaguely familiar tranquility. She would have liked to do more sorting in the morning, but decided not to push it with another sick day and, anyway, she liked the idea of all the work left to do here. The house needed her.

§

At about three AM an extraordinary thing happened. The dream was back, almost familiar now—the windswept mountain ridge, the light breeze on her face, the lush colors of spring. The silent, secret man at the edge of the canyon. Determined to see his face, Kat approached him, but as she neared she heard *Somewhere My Love* in the tinny tones of Ruth's music box and woke with a start, her confusion as to where she was compounded by the fact that the song continued to play. She switched on the light and looked at the dresser, and the lid to the music box was open.

Oh, dear.

She wished her robe were on the chair by the bed, where it would normally be if she hadn't just been working on the "everything in its place" matter. She jumped out of bed and found it in the closet, pulling it on as quickly as she could, then quietly lowered the lid on the music box. She looked cautiously out into the hallway. "Is someone there?" she said, her voice hoarse with fear as she clutched her robe to her throat. But no one was, which she confirmed by checking every corner of the house.

When she returned to bed and switched off the light the music box on the dresser was barely lit from the streetlight filtering through the curtains. She watched it until she fell back asleep.

eight

Kat was up at six and made her first cup of coffee in her new house. She toasted and buttered a muffin, and took it to the bedroom to eat while she dressed, pausing several times to consider the music box on the dresser. *Weird.*

She was pretty sure Jason would want to meet with her that day and carefully considered what to wear. Kat's feelings about Jason were complicated, not surprising since Kat's feelings about men she found attractive and interesting usually were. He made her feel fluttery, arousing a kind of primal déjà vu that might even predate the hundreds of fairy tales and romance novels she'd digested since she'd been a little girl. Or maybe the stories were a symptom, maybe he just made her feel safe, like he could be the protector she'd been waiting for since The Darkness (the pre-adolescent period represented in her memory solely by the fiction she'd escaped to so desperately her teacher warned her mother it was hurting her grades). She settled on a tight black light wool skirt that just grazed her knees, heels a little higher than she usually wore to work (running shoes for the bus ride) and a fitted white cotton blouse, the buttons pulling slightly across her chest. Of course she wore a black wool blazer over it, the bus ride was strange enough without looking like a porn librarian, although the running shoes probably took care of that.

Kat brushed her teeth, momentarily considering changing her blouse as she looked at the straining buttons on her chest. What if Jason wanted her in that way? First, they work together and MartCo's rules about executive fraternization were positively medieval. Secondly, there was Tina's Dictum #1 (or maybe #2 or #3, Kat had lost count): "Never have a boyfriend or a car cooler than you are." And, third… There was a third there somewhere.

The bus ride to work was pleasantly uneventful, but, indeed, now required a transfer, and Kat thought again about having her car fixed. *I mean, what is the problem? Focus, right? Screw the same astral plain,* she thought, *I'd settle for the same planet.*

Tina was late, as usual, arriving just as Kat returned to her cubicle from a coffee run to the vending machine. "Wow, you look hot. If Max sees your ass in that skirt he'll have a heart attack. How was the bus?"

"No one showed me their genitals. But I have to transfer now. I barely made it on time. I'm seriously thinking of getting my car fixed. It's just about focus, right?"

"Focus and not being murderous," said Tina as she went to her cubicle.

"I beg your pardon?" Kat said, annoyed, as she sat down at her desk. She opened Outlook and about a hundred and fifty emails loaded. She dialed her mother on her cell as she scrolled through them, marking the ones she needed to reply to immediately. The call rang six times, then Jean's answering machine picked up. *Effing caller ID.* Kat waited impatiently through her mother's awkwardly recorded greeting. *Yes, I know you're not there (BS). Yes, I know my message is important to you (as if). Yes, I know to wait for the beep before leaving it.*

"Hi, mom, it's me. I really want to talk to you." said Kat when the machine finally indicated it was ready for her message. "I'm sorry you're upset. This isn't about you. Call me please."

She closed the phone. Speaking of complicated, Kat's relationship with her mother was twisted and probably couch-worthy. She tried to remember if there had been a time when Jean hadn't been unhappy and depressed (the well-used boxes of wine in the fridge didn't seem to help), or if they had any relatives she wasn't angry with. Ruth had been her twin, and Jean hadn't spoken with her in at least twenty years, and went postal the few times Kat had dared to mention her name. Ditto about Kat's father, who had simply left one day, never to be heard from again. *I can't imagine why*, thought Kat as she returned to her Sisyphean task. She thought about calling Jason to see if he wanted to meet with her today, then remembered the "third": Rebecca's warning about him. Was that really about Kat, or was Rebecca projecting her own stuff on her?

…The fire crackled in the stone fireplace, freshly split oak logs spitting tiny Roman candles against the screen. Jason, in a white T-shirt, jeans and thick wooly crew socks, was napping on the over-sized leather sofa, an open leather-bound volume in his lap. Kat came quietly in from the kitchen with two glasses of red wine, her tousled hair falling softly around her shoulders, wearing his big warm flannel shirt over a white lace balconette bra and matching panties. She put his glass on the low table, careful not to wake her lover, but he surprised her, pulling him down to him.

"Careful," she giggled, "I'll spill my wine."

"Well, we can't have that, can we?" he said, taking it from her and placing the glass beside his own. Then he kissed her, the deepest, hottest kiss two lovers ever shared in the history of the world…

The phone on Kat's desk jangled, and she answered, "Kat Young." It was Jason. "I was just thinking about you," she said, slightly disoriented.

"Something good, I hope," he said.

"Uh, wondering if you want to try to meet today?"

"Will you be free anytime after three?" he asked.

"Let me check my calendar," said Kat, not bothering to check anything. "Uh, yes, how's four-thirty?"

"Four-thirty's fine. See you then," he said, and rang off abruptly. *Efficiently*, thought Kat as she hung up the phone. Like a man who doesn't waste time wondering what he wants. She couldn't imagine Jason waffling over what to order in a Chinese restaurant.

Three hours and nearly a hundred emails later, Kat tried calling the regional manager Rebecca wanted her to fire. She wasn't in the office (troubling), but Kat managed to get her assistant, who was at first reluctant to say anything, to open up a bit, and the girl confirmed that her boss had just separated from her husband and was, indeed, going through a very bad patch. Saying as little as possible so as not to freak everybody out, Kat asked the assistant to please pick up the slack as much as possible, and to call her if there was anything she could do to help. As she hung up her stomach rumbled, and she decided to eat at her desk again, since Tina had gone to lunch early, saying she had a date, and to make up for the time lost to her meeting with Jason that afternoon.

Kat walked into the lunchroom, wondering to herself that Tina had the girl power to get a guy to come downtown to have lunch with her. She was bent over trying to read the expiration date on a turkey sandwich in the machine when she heard a gurgling sound from the doorway and turned just in time to see Max, who immediately turned tail and disappeared down the hall. "Max!" she called after him. "I'm over it." She turned back to the machine, muttering to herself, "I'm not a mean person." Then she remembered what Tina had said about her ass in this skirt, and wondered if he'd taken another picture.

She pulled the lever on the machine, thinking how it was like a slot machine where winning meant not going to the hospital, and the sandwich dropped into the tray. She picked it up and looked at the date. *Today. We have a winner!*

As she left the room she checked out her butt in the reflection from the glass door.

§

At four-twenty-eight Kat stepped off the elevator on Jason's floor carrying her iPad, relieved to not see the secretary, or whatever she was, with the superior attitude. She rapped lightly on the slightly ajar door to his office, and Jason said, "Come in!"

Kat entered cautiously. He was on the phone, but indicated for her to sit as he continued his conversation.

"We can absolutely be ready."

Kat went to the sofa, pausing to take in the view before sitting down.

"That's our edge, they won't expect us to be. They've got to think we're still six months from roll-out." He smiled at Kat. "Look, I've got somebody here. I'll call you when I've had a chance to review the numbers."

He hung up and leaned back in his chair, looking at her over steepled fingers.

"I'm moving the Seattle meeting up to next week. Want to come?"

Kat hesitated, surprised. "Wow, I, uh, sure. That would be great."

"I said I wanted you on board, why not all the way?"

"I don't know if I can be ready," said Kat.

"I know you can," Jason said, as he got to his feet. "In fact, I have total confidence you can do it." He pushed the door closed and sat next to her. "Your prelim work helped me get this prioritized.

"Is Rebecca OK with this?" Kat, noticed Stevens was looking at her curiously. "What? Do I have ink on my face?"

"No, it's just that you've just got such beautiful eyes. I haven't been able to stop thinking about them."

"What?" said Kat, not sure she'd heard him correctly. Also, she'd noticed he hadn't been looking at her eyes.

"Your eyes, they're amazing." He raised his hands to her face and gently removed her glasses, then leaned in and kissed her on the mouth.

It may not have been the deepest, hottest kiss in the history of the world, but it was definitely a kiss. "Is this real?" said Kat, pulling away slightly.

"What do you mean?" said Jason, his hands on her shoulders now, pulling her in for another.

"Uh, I have to go," she said, jumping to her feet. "I'm sorry, I…" Having absolutely no idea what to say, she decided to say nothing and went to the door, light-headed enough to wobble slightly on her heels.

"Kat," Jason said as her hand reached the doorknob. She stopped. He looked really worried. "You won't, uh, say anything about this, will you?"

§

When Kat got back to her cube she threw herself into her chair dramatically enough to get Tina's attention. "Are you OK?" she said, her head appearing over the divider.

"I don't know," said Kat. "I just had an out of body experience."

The irony of this statement wasn't lost on her. She'd entertained something of a generic fantasy of being swept up in the strong arms of a dashing hero for a long time, and not just with Jason. So it actually happens and it doesn't seem real. *Perfect*.

"How was your lunch date?" asked Kat. Tina still hadn't gotten back when she had gone upstairs to meet with Jason, which was crazy, because Tina was definitely on Rebecca's list.

"The guy's hot, smitten, and wrapped," Tina said, holding up her little finger to indicate where. "Oh, by the way, you'd never guess who just called me."

"No idea," said Kat, still reeling from her "meeting" with Jason.

"Marty," said Tina, the disgust clear in her voice.

"Oh, God, I forgot all about that."

"You knew he was going to ask me out?"

"Sort of. I mean, it was so ridiculous anyway."

"No kidding. Is he on drugs?"

"Just uncut stupidity. What did you say?"

"I called him scum, told him to go fuck himself and hung up. Are you sure you're OK?"

"I'm fine. It's just been a crazy day."

"Do you want a ride home?" said Tina.

"Thanks, Teen, but I've got some stuff I need to sort out in my head, and I'd rather save the favor for when I need it."

"There's no favor quota, GF," said Tina, and disappeared back into her cubicle.

§

Kat worked till seven, not only because she still hadn't caught up with everything, but because she didn't want to risk seeing Jason on her way out of the building. Of course when the elevator doors opened he was on it. He smiled weakly as she got on. Neither said anything during the long ride to the lobby. Kat got off first and made it out the main doors before Jason called out to her. "Wait," he said, and she stopped and waited for him to catch up to her. "Kat, I am so sorry."

"Yeah, well, hmmm…" She looked at him thoughtfully. "Walk me to the bus?"

"Let me drive you home," he said.

"That's not necessary," said Kat, resuming her walk to the street, "the bus is fine."

"You probably think I, I mean, I've never done anything like that before."

"I'm sure."

"No really," he protested.

"It's OK, I believe you. Look, Jason, I like you and I'm flattered. I'm just worried about the whole office thing. I mean, we could be fired."

"No, absolutely, you're right, it's crazy. I'm just glad you're not, you know…"

"We're adults," Kat said. "Adults deal with things in an adult manner. But I love that you want me on your team. I mean, you still do, right?"

Jason said, "Absolutely! I have total confidence in your abilities."

Of course, this was the tricky part. Kat would never know if that were true, because for him to say otherwise could be grounds for some very nasty legal stuff. She decided it didn't matter; she would go five extra miles to be worthy of his trust. Kat stopped at the corner waiting for the light.

"That's where I catch it," she said, pointing across the street.

"I'll walk you there," he said.

"I'll be OK from here. I'm glad we talked like, you know, adults."

"Like adults," he said.

"Right," said Kat hesitating. "Well…" She went in for an awkward hug, which he returned awkwardly. She could see a bus approaching. The light turned green and the Walk sign flashed. "There's my bus," she said. "I'll get the report done ASAP." She crossed the street. Was he watching her? And if he was, was he looking at her ass in this stupid skirt? She was afraid to look back. When she got to the bus bench and turned around he was gone.

§

Having less than a week to prepare for the presentation was actually perfect for Kat, because it allowed her to do what she'd done since she was a little girl to avoid dealing with troubling matters: work. That night she pulled the first of a planned series of all-nighters, collapsing into bed at four-thirty AM. And it almost worked; she only found herself thinking about The Kiss twice. OK, maybe three times.

When her alarm sounded interrupting her two hours of dreamless sleep she woke once again disoriented, still not used to waking up in her new house. She looked at the quiet music box, now not sure if it hadn't been a dream. She thought about The Kiss.

One thing about sleep deprivation is you can pretty well sleepwalk through your day, although when she boarded the bus, Kat had a disconcerting moment when she couldn't remember if she'd gotten dressed after her shower. But she had it (the bus) down now. Three words: noise-canceling headphones. That and make eye contact with no one. There'd been moments since she started taking it when she'd wavered, almost made the call to the shop storing her car to tell them to go ahead and fix it. But one thing she was really good at was finishing something once she started it, and she wasn't ready to cave, especially now another Friday was here and only one fellow bus rider all week had shown her his penis.

Rebecca had grudgingly signed off on Seattle, and at five that afternoon Jason welcomed Kat back to his office and introduced her to Taylor Brown, the financial analyst member of their little team, who would be crunching the numbers. She presented her preliminary DMF (Developmental Framework) for the project and Jason and Taylor declared themselves suitably impressed, both requesting copies. Kat said she had more work to do, but Taylor insisted he needed to start crunching, so she promised she'd email them what she had as soon as she got back to her office. It was going to be a long weekend and, after catching the faintest wisp of cedar and verbena when Jason leaned over the table to review Taylor's numbers, she could see getting The Kiss out of her mind wasn't going to be as easy as simply working harder. Although in this case having no social life (or as Tina described her, no life period) would at least keep the distractions to a minimum.

§

Getting off the bus at her corner she checked the Starbucks parking lot for Cooper's truck as usual, but it hadn't been there all week. There'd been no art show invite left in her mailbox either. *Stupid to say I'm not ready to date*, she thought, then remembered The Kiss. Damn, she was jumping out of her skin.

Kat opened a bottle of Chardonnay and made herself a salad, eating it and sipping wine standing by the counter in the kitchen. *At least I'm not eating straight from the fridge with the door open.* Then The Kiss intruded again. *What if he is The One?* What if he could fill the hole she'd felt in her heart since The Darkness, and she'd pushed him away because of something as trivial as losing a job she cared less and less about every day? She'd fixated on the vent over her desk again that morning when she'd first come to work, imagining it was her only source of air and it was pumping out carbon monoxide and everyone on her floor would be blue and dead when the rescue teams arrived.

At five AM Saturday morning she fell into bed without reviewing any of her work and slept like she was dead until almost noon. Staggering into the kitchen she made herself a latté to wash down an egg-topped muffin, then sat down with a second cup of coffee and opened her laptop and the DMF file. It was good; it was really good. Funny how someone with Jason's education, experience and position couldn't imagine the total geometry of a business plan. *It's a chick thing*, she smiled to herself. *Now if Taylor can make the numbers work.*

The problem was now she had the entire weekend with no mind-numbing work to escape to, and The Kiss was seriously troubling her, the thought that she may have turned her back on her one chance for happiness, like she wouldn't recognize Prince Charming if she hit him with her car. She tried taking refuge in her usual safe zones. She baked two batches of cookies, oatmeal, a white bread recipe she embellished with multi-colored jumbo raisins (on first taste people acted like she'd invented fire), and coconut macaroons she'd found on a new cooking site. The combined scents as they were cooling engendered a strange reaction, an intense nostalgia that led to sobbing tears. *I'm losing my mind*, thought Kat, munching on a tear-soaked macaroon.

She took the cookies and coffee (her fourth cup of the day) to the study, the floor still cluttered with boxes of books waiting for clear shelf space. The problem was it felt weird taking down her aunt's books. And anyway she felt like she should read them. She selected the book Cooper had said was one of the best he'd ever read, Flaubert's Sentimental Education (or in this case *L'Éducation sentimentale*, since it was the French edition) from the shelf. But it was in French. She reshelved it, feeling stupid. She caught sight of herself in the oak-framed mirror on the far wall. *Thirty years old and you only speak English.* Then she wondered if she should cut her hair. *But it's already almost too short to tousle*, she thought, smiling grimly at her own joke. *What difference does it make?* she thought, completing her downward spiral into the dumps. *I'm never going to be a tousled romance heroine.*

Kat recognized a familiar blue spine in one of the boxes and picked up *Welyn Warrior*, a paperback she'd read at least six times. She pushed a box aside and sat down on the floor. Back to the wall, she turned to the first page and escaped to where dreams come true. Three hours later, coffee and macaroons long since exhausted, she hadn't moved, except to turn the pages. The first time she'd read the book she'd stopped at this point and jealously counted the pages remaining, but now she accepted the inevitable and raced through to the end:

Her golden mane wrapped in a warrior's scarf, Rhiannon ran amongst the battlements, firing arrows from the baskets left by each crenel for the now frantically absent guards. The gentry were gone as well, turned tail to save their plump asses, taking only the fewest servants so they might travel light as they fled the Welyn, whom they knew would likely roast them alive if captured. Rhiannon had for a moment hoped she might have been included in their party, since the baron had taken her so often, and with such relish. It had become a joke among his daughters, who considered her tall lean figure and strong angular face hideously ugly beside their beautiful porcine roundness, and whose sneering demands Rhiannon hated as much as she did the lord himself. The irony of this latter fury was that she had once hoped for the slightest kindness from him, not only to survive her ordeal, but out of the hidden need still burning in her from the loss of her father, but he'd shown only contempt for her once his grotesque lust had been satisfied.

And now she fought an enemy she didn't know and couldn't see. Valiantly and well, it seemed, because none had dared cross the meadow below since their first onslaught had been repelled by the hail of arrows she'd unleashed on them, leaving many dead and wounded. The small fortress' abutment of the cliffs

141

behind it was one of the few things Rhiannon was grateful for besides the ample supply of arrows. But now darkness had fallen and there was movement in the shadows, which allowed barely enough light for her to discern their barbaric antlered helmets, or were they actual monsters with horns growing from their skulls? She'd never seen one of the fearsome creatures the Olwyn described as grotesquely ugly. Dreading the moment when she'd be faced with the answer to this question, a moment she knew was inevitable, Rhiannon scrambled to another crenel, staying low to avoid the arrows that occasionally whispered through the air above her, answering her own in deadly conversation.

Then all was quiet. But, soon enough, she knew they'd be on the move again. *A fool's errand*, she thought, *a fool's end*. By occupying the invaders she was giving the Olwyn, the people she despised, the gift of time, now the same as the gift of life, in exchange for her own. But something in her, something she hadn't even known she possessed burned within her: a warrior's heart, and now for the first time she felt alive and free.

Movement below! In a flash five arrows flew from her bow into the darkness, and she heard the soft moans of the wounded and the rustle as they were dragged back into the dark forest. She held her fire, fingering the pommel above the hilt of the Baron's broadsword which hung from her hip. In the haste of the cowards' departure many such weapons had been left behind, and she had chosen the finest among them. The surprise was how light it had felt in her hands, remembering how the Baron needed his servants even to attach it to his waist, let alone wield it in anger. Light and deadly, as she swung it in a graceful arc over her head, then traced a line in the air where a man's heart might beat. A man or a Welyn.

Soon they would realize there was but a single archer manning the battlement. Soon they would come. She laughed to herself as she imagined their faces when they realized not only was it a single archer, but a scullery maid whore who had thinned their ranks for the better part of a day, and well into the night. Then *soon* came. A grappling hook sailed over the rampart and slid back to lock into place, followed by another in the adjacent crenel, then another. Rhiannon knew if she leaned over the battlement to use her bow she'd be instantly skewered by a dozen arrows. *So this is it*, she thought, notching what she knew might be her last arrow and resting it on the bow's shelf. Pulling the bowstring to its fullest extension she waited until the Welyn lifted himself onto the wall, then released it, piercing his heart. The man (for indeed, that's what he was) hesitated for a moment, wearing a look of surprise, as much as from the revelation of who his attacker was as from his awareness that he was dying. A second appeared in the adjacent crenel, and was as quickly dispatched. But now more hooks flew over the ramparts, slid back and locked, and soon a horned helmet appeared in every crenel and Rhiannon tossed the bow aside and rested her hand on the thick, leather-wrapped hilt of the broadsword. There was no question of living, but she would certainly take as many with her as she could to the heaven or hell awaiting scullery maids and whores.

Now eight men had pulled themselves over the wall and stood before her, looking around them, surprised to see the "army" that had held them at bay. The first laughed, then the others joined in as men continued to pour over the wall, wondering at what their compatriots could find amusing in this deadly venture. Still Rhiannon rested her hand on the sword, favoring surprise. She studied them, not only for weakness, but because it was the first time in her adult life she'd been among humans taller than herself. The first advanced on her, speaking a language familiar sounding but unintelligible to her ears. He pointed at her weapon and spoke again, his tone demanding. She waited till he was close enough she could feel the heat from his body, then drew the sword from its scabbard in a sweeping motion and detached his head.

A shocked silence spread through the throng as the headless torso teetered and collapsed under the weight of its armor. Then a dozen broadswords were drawn as the warriors exploded in anger and fell on the lone girl, who responded with a blind fury, cutting them down one by one like a woodsman wielding a well-honed axe through a stand of fated trees, till only one stood. She lowered her sword, waiting, in the tactic that had served her well in the mayhem.

Now somewhat accustomed to the features of the Welyn, even though she had just cut down eleven of them like so many weeds, she studied his face, surprised to find it nice looking, comely even. His hair was as blond as her own, but he made no attempt to control it; it spilled from his helmet like the feathers of a golden willow. He raised his sword for the attack, but she didn't tense, waiting for the moment when she would sweep him from the earth. But the attack didn't come. Lowering his sword he pointed to a spot on his neck. For the first time her certainty faltered. Was he asking to have his head removed?

"Raise your blade," she demanded. "Attack me if you have the courage of your friends."

"Why do you fight us?" he said in the language of the Olwyn. "And why do you speak the language of the pigs?"

"What do you mean?" she said, refusing to let her guard down.

"You are Welyn," he said.

Still Rhiannon held her stance, prepared to dispatch this giant of a man as quickly as she had his brothers.

"Have you never seen your own people?" he said, aware that the slightest threatening movement would spring her to action.

In fact, she hadn't, at least at an age that allowed remembering. But now for the first time in her life of anguish and strife she felt a stirring deep in her soul. Was this only because these men resembled her so strongly? Or was there something else about this man? She suddenly realized he was staring fixedly at her neck, at the same time lowering his sword slightly. His guard was down! Till then she'd fought defensively, but now she saw the opportunity to strike. She flew at him, her sword a blur as it arced toward his neck. But the seasoned warrior reacted instinctively, and her blade found only his in a violent metallic clash of steel. He locked her weapon with his own, his face close to hers, and swept it from her hands as if he were taking a toy from a child. Then he tore the wrap from her head and gripped her hair. She could feel the heat of his oiled muscles, the faint sweetness of his breath on her jaw, as he twisted her head away from him. She prepared to die.

"At least give me a warrior's mercy," she hissed, when a moment later she realized she was alive. "End it!"

But still the man let her live. Holding her firmly by the thatch of thick blond hair in his fist, he turned her head, and pushed back the golden locks that fell to his shoulders. "Do you see?" he said.

Rhiannon did, and was shocked at what she saw: a tiny glyph tattooed behind his jaw. Shocked because the same mark was on her neck, a mark that had been upon her when she'd been found abandoned in the fields of the Olwyn, and her hand went automatically to it. "What does this mean?" she whispered. Everything she knew about the world had turned upside down since the morning, and here was yet another paradigm shift.

"That you are Rhiannon of the Menw, and my betrothed since we were babes."

"I don't understand," she said, aware that more Welyn were pouring over the wall. Most launched into searches of the fortress, but several gathered around them and for the first time she was afraid they might not just kill her.

"I am Ansgar. I was chosen for you and you for me in the first moon of our birth, and for this reason we could never have another. My father told me your clan was attacked and all were killed before your first year. Till now I believed I'd always walk alone."

Rhiannon's mind raced, thoughts of escape struggling with something she'd never felt before, something you and I take for granted: hope.

"Will you release me then?" she ventured. She didn't like being held by her hair, like a kitten in its mother's jaws. At the same time, she wasn't sure what the other men would do if she weren't dangling in the paw of this giant.

"No," he said. His reply didn't surprise her, but what occurred next did; he pulled her face to his own and kissed her hard on the mouth, the first passionate kiss she had ever experienced. For a moment she struggled against it, then, lightheaded, the earth moved, her heart soaring in a way she never felt possible, and she…

…*pushed him away, reminding him they could be fired for fraternizing*, thought Kat, adding her own twist to the story as she snapped the book shut. Then she relived The Kiss for the umpteenth time since that fateful moment in Jason's office.

nine

Kat knew something major was up when she got to her office and there was a voicemail from Rebecca excusing her from what Tina referred to as RMT (Rebecca Monday Torture) because of <u>Mr.</u> Stevens' project (note emphasis on Mr.). She'd planned on waiting till after Rebecca's meeting to deliver her work to Jason, but went straight up to his office, encountering Tina on the way, who was apoplectic with jealousy. Not about Jason, about not having to waste her morning in Rebecca's meeting.

Jason's door was open. He was at his desk, the snotty girl she'd encountered earlier leaning over him as they discussed some finer point of a document, her skirt so tight it threatened to cut off the circulation to her legs. "*If Jason turns his head too suddenly his nose will be in her cleavage*, Kat thought as she knocked lightly. Jason brightened visibly when he saw her. "Kat, come in, come in. This is Meredith, she's kind of a floating admin assistant for the department," he said, then, to the girl, "This is Kat Young, our other team member on Seattle." Jason looked at Kat. "We were just going over Taylor's report. How's yours coming along?"

"Done," Kat smiled. "I emailed you the file just before I came up. It should be in your inbox."

Jason checked his mail. "And…there it is," he said. "I'll forward it to Taylor. Meredith, will you please give him a heads up on that, and can you come back at eleven when I've had a chance to review it for notes?"

"Absolutely, Mr. Stevens," she said, Kat noting that it was MR. Stevens now for her as well. She gave Kat a tight smile. "Nice to meet you." She paused at the door to ask Jason if he wanted it closed.

"No, Meredith, thanks," he said, "you can leave it open."

At this Kat decided they needed to clear the air. "Jason, I want to say something about Friday."

"It's not necessary. I got it; I was completely out of line. Kat, I have the greatest respect for you, both as a co-worker and a woman. Right now the only focus we need to have is on Seattle."

"Well, OK. Good," Kat said, although that wasn't what she'd had in mind.

"First," Jason said, "Meredith is booking our flights today."

"All right then," said Kat, "all systems go!" *What am I saying?*

"Better than go," said Jason. "Mr. Martin was blown away by your DMF."

"It wasn't done," she said. Hearing her rough draft had been read by the CEO brought her neatly down to earth.

"It was plenty far along enough to paint the picture I was looking for. Not only is he fully on board, we, I mean you, me and Taylor, are doing a presentation for him and several board members."

That explained Rebecca. "When?" Kat said. "Taylor hasn't even seen my completed DMF."

"Tomorrow afternoon." Jason said. "Don't worry, he's good and he's fast."

A mild panic swept over Kat, the pop-quiz anxiety of the unprepared adolescent. "Is there anything you want me to do?"

"You've done it. We'll meet with Taylor to fine tune and prepare our dog and pony show."

"But you haven't read it yet," said Kat.

"I looked it over before I sent it to Taylor."

"I was standing here," said Kat.

"I'm a fast study. I'm sure it's great. If I have any questions I'll call you this afternoon."

§

Kat sat down at her desk thinking, *Well, that's that. I'll either get promoted or I'll be worrying about how I'm going to pay my property taxes.* On the other hand, everyone else in her department was still stuck in Stuckie's meeting and, except for her meeting with Jason and Taylor Tuesday morning and the frightening prospect of the presentation, she had almost three whole days to actually do her job, which meant she could conceivably be caught up for the first time in six years.

Tina came dragging back just before lunch. "It was a living hell," she said. "Without you there, she was asking me questions, like, every three minutes. I mean, I got zero sleep."

"Well, let that be a lesson; I may not be here forever to protect you," said Kat.

"Don't say that, even as a joke. It was too horrible for words. I have to get some lunch; I'm starving."

"I'll join you," said Kat, shutting off her monitor.

"No kidding?" said a genuinely surprised Tina. "You're not going to stay chained to your desk and play tuna roulette?"

"I'm actually getting caught up without Rebecca breathing down my neck. Is that gourmet taco truck still parking on Beverly?"

"Yes! I'm in, just let me get my purse." Tina dove into her cubicle and was back in a flash, practically panting like a dog promised a walk.

"Let's get Nita too," said Kat, following her up the aisle. They stopped in Juanita's doorway.

"You up for some Wolfgang Puck tacos?" said Tina.

152

"Thank you Jesus," said Juanita, grabbing her purse. "If I looked at that thing another minute my stomach was gonna' fire my eyes."

§

It was a perfect summer day, the brilliant blue unmarred by even the tiniest cloud. When they walked out onto the street Kat filled her lungs as she always did when freed from the ventilator above her desk, as if she had just emerged from a submarine that had been traveling under the polar ice. Their truck was there, and with nearly no line. Kat and Tina ordered Java Tacos, Juanita a sauce-slavered meatball sandwich and two orders of truffle fries. And ketchup. Then they found a couple of planters where they could sit and scarf.

"So what the eff is going on?" said Tina as she savored the first bite of her taco.

"What do you mean?" said Kat, still adding sauce from a tiny plastic tub.

"You were like the eight-hundred pound gorilla at the meeting this morning."

"Thanks," said Kat.

"You know what I mean. So you've had, like, six meetings with him. And you can't tell us you didn't have a thing for him."

"Kat and Jason sitting in a tree, k...i...s...s...i...n...g," Juanita said, looking lovingly at her fries.

Kat was sure there was no way they knew anything about what had happened on Friday; Jason had clearly been mortified, and certainly wouldn't have said anything about it to anyone. But she felt like she had to throw them a bone. Anyway she had to talk about it to someone and they were her best friends. "OK," she said, "I wrote this proposal, like, six months ago? And Jason, I mean, Mr. Stevens..."

"Jason," interrupted Tina.

"OK, Jason," said Kat, feeling herself blush slightly at the word. "Anyway, he saw it and I guess showed it to Mr. Martin and they greenlit it, with me on board," she said, making air quotes around "on board." Kat shrugged, "It's all happened pretty fast." She left out the part about the meeting with Mr. Martin and the board members. It was already feeling a little puffy.

"When's Seattle?" asked Tina.

Kat smiled, "Thursday."

"Oh, my God," said Juanita, wiping ketchup from her lips. "This is better than the Sex In The City Two or Three movie, or whichever one they're on now. You have to tell us every single detail of the entire trip. I mean everything."

"This is about work. I'm not going there for, you know," said Kat, thinking, *Am I really this transparent?*

"Uh huh," said Juanita, unconvinced. "Every single detail, you hear me?"

§

Kat was pretty sure there wouldn't be any details of the kind that would interest Juanita, but things with Jason's "team" went very well. When Taylor finished his numbers they were nearly the same as Kat's projections. Meredith emailed her Jason's notes, but Kat sent her revisions directly back to him, not trusting the "floating admin assistant." Tuesday afternoon's presentation to Mr. Martin (no board members were present) went swimmingly. The CEO asked her several personal questions. Not terribly personal, of course, just the sort one might be asked when one was being considered for a more important position with the company. Packing for her trip Wednesday night she felt an odd kind of peace and confidence. She looked around the bedroom at the now familiar objects. The house had been lucky for her. OK, maybe not romantically, but she felt oddly fulfilled, especially considering only a few weeks before this she'd felt her job was as suffocating as her relationship with what's-his-name. Now she felt like she was on the verge of actually going somewhere, even if it was just Seattle.

That night the dream returned. Once again she was on a windswept ridge in the Santa Monica Mountains, behind a tall figure of a man, his face hidden. And, again, the dream ended with his face still a mystery. Could he be Jason?

ten

...President and General Manager Kat Young, wearing a sleek black Valentino suit and black patent Loubitains with red lipstick heels, stepped onto the drop down stairs of the Global US corporate jet, its starboard engine already purring quietly in anticipation. She smiled quietly to herself knowing Senior VP Jason Stevens was right behind her and would be admiring the tight curves of her perfect ass in the tight, smooth wool of the perfectly fitting skirt, to say nothing of her tight calves in the nearly four-inch heels. It had become a kind of foreplay for them, behaving in a coolly professional manner among the employees, then tearing into each other like savage starving beasts when they were alone.

"Good morning, Ms. Young," the flight attendant smiled. "Good morning, Mr. Stevens."

Kat and Jason made their way to the soft, deep leather seats as the girl raised the stairs and the pilot fired up the port engine, its shrill whine answered by its sister's as the sleek craft began to taxi.

"I'll serve the coffee as soon as we're in the air," said the flight attendant, buckling her shoulder harness for her backwards-facing seat. Kat smiled again, having experienced the girl's professionalism on each leg of their tour; she would be served a creamy latté, Jason caffé Americano.

The engines whine became a scream and the little plane vaulted into the air, pressing them back into their seats as they circled the Milan airport and settled into a westerly course. *Paris*, thought Kat. Was there a more romantic word? They hadn't been there since they'd first worked together at MartCo. She closed her eyes and it was as if it had been only yesterday when they'd made frantic, passionate love in the tiny hotel room as the rain beat against the window panes. Then riding to the top of the Eifel Tower, sated on sex, food and wine, where he had held her in the wind, high above the city of lights.

As the flight attendant unbuckled her seatbelt and set to work preparing the coffee, Kat looked at Jason, who smiled back, a smile that never failed to make her heart soar. He was close enough she felt the warmth of his body, sensed the faintest touch of verbena and cedar.

Were they really fooling anyone? Surely even a fool could see that they lived and breathed for each other. The girl brought their coffees, his café Americano, her latté, and he lifted his cup and she waited for the words she longed to hear. "We have begun our descent into the Seattle area," he said, his voice slightly gay and tinged with feedback...

The flight attendant adjusted the volume level, then brought the microphone back to his lips. "Please bring your seatbacks to their full upright and locked position, turn off any electronic devices and stow computers and carry-on items in the overhead compartment or under the seat in front of you."

Kat brought her seatback up, then nudged Taylor, who was dozing in the middle seat.

"Wha...?" he mumbled.

"We're landing in Seattle," she said, and smiled at Jason, who was in the window seat, in his shirt sleeves, his tie loosened. She hadn't seen him like this before, casual, that is. She liked it.

Taylor groaned.

"You OK?" asked Jason.

"I don't know," said Taylor, "I feel a little weird."

§

The three wheeled their carry-on bags to the luggage area, recognizing their car service driver by his shabby livery and hand-lettered sign reading, "Jason Stevens."

Taylor looked bad enough as the limo pulled into airport traffic that Jason asked him if he was going to make it.

"Absolutely," said Taylor. "I'm just a little queasy. I think it might have been the sausage biscuit I had at the airport."

"Do you want to stop for a soda or Pepto or something?" asked Kat.

"I'll be fine, let's just run the numbers, they're my Pepto," he said, opening his briefcase and bringing out the spreadsheet. Jason didn't look convinced.

Taylor seemed to rally when the driver dropped them off at the granite and glass office building for their scheduled meeting. They'd gone straight from the airport, so still had their suitcases, in addition to their computers and briefcases.

They wheeled their bags to the elevator. Kat straightened Taylor's tie and patted his shoulder. "You're OK, right?"

"Good to go," he said, his face ashen as the doors opened.

They trooped on and Jason pressed the button for the sixty-eighth floor. As the car accelerated, Taylor steadied himself with a hand on the side rail. Aware that both Kat and Jason were looking at him, he gave them a thumbs-up.

The plan was for a three-stage PowerPoint presentation. Kat would begin, laying out the proposal's broad strokes, Taylor would crunch the numbers, and Jason would swoop in for the kill. Since she'd been a little girl, Kat had been terrified of anything resembling public speaking. Her barely audible responses had been a running joke in school. She hated speaking in Rebecca's meetings, but it was unavoidable. Her solution was to be overly prepared, to take such a huge information dump when Rebecca called on her that no one dared ask a follow up question. She'd chosen a similar approach to this situation, a large part of the reason Jason was so impressed with her work. But she felt strangely calm now, and not just because her DMF was perfect; having Jason there completed her in a strange way she'd never felt before.

The conference room, with floor-to-ceiling windows offering a panoramic view of the Puget Sound, had a polished ebony table, long enough to accommodate a meeting with thirty people, but only three faced them in the opposing chairs. Taylor, the official team nerd, set up the projector for the presentation as introductions were made. There was a definite uncertainty and tension in their host's demeanor, tempered with a careful professionalism. All of which would have normally scared the hell out of Kat, but when her moment came she stood and began

161

with only the slightest hesitation and elevated pulse, much more aware of Jason's presence than the enemy's.

"First of all, I'd like to thank you for giving us the opportunity to present our proposal for this exciting project to you today," Kat began. "Our companies, each preeminent in its own field, joined together have the potential to be not only a national leader in marketing and management, but an international one as well."

There was a slight choking sound behind her as Kat clicked the remote to change the screen. Taylor wore a puzzled expression, as if he didn't recognize her. Then he projectile vomited on the beautiful table.

§

Kat was sitting beside Taylor when he woke up on a leather couch in the reception area. "Taylor?" she asked gently, her hand on his shoulder. "How do you feel?"

He covered his face with his arm and moaned. "Like I was hit by a bus. What happened?"

"Uh, you got sick?"

"I know that part. Did I ruin everything?"

"Actually, I think we got a little sympathy action out of it. It was definitely the most 3D PowerPoint presentation they've ever seen. Do you want to go to the ER?"

"No, I'm actually feeling a little better." He tried to sit up. "Where's Jason?"

"He's finishing up." she said. "Just lie there for another minute, the hotel is sending a car over for us."

§

Kat waited with Taylor as Jason checked in at the front desk and got their key cards. "The rooms are all upper floors and I got us views," he said. He gave them their keys as they followed him to the elevators.

"God, I love winning," said Jason as he pressed the up button. "What a rush."

"You were unbelievable," gushed Kat. "It was like you were reading their minds or something."

"No, you were unbelievable," Jason said as the elevator doors opened. "Do you have a photographic memory for numbers or something?"

"Unbelievable," Taylor mumbled to himself as he dragged himself into the elevator.

"I know this great place near the Pike Street Market that does unbelievable fish," Jason said as he pressed the buttons for their floors. "Meet in the lobby in an hour?"

Taylor stared at the key envelope as if it were a moon rock that had just floated into his hand. "I'm just gonna' check the mini bar for seltzer and catch some porn." The doors opened for his floor and he staggered off. "You guys have fun."

Kat and Jason's rooms were on the same floor. "Lobby in an hour for amazing fish," he said, saluting her with his key envelope.

Kat's room was quietly modern and elegant, and the view was everything Jason promised. *Jason promised*, she thought. She like the sound of those words bumping into each other. She opened her suitcase and took out a beige silk blouse, tan slacks and navy blazer, which she arranged on the bed like a version of herself. The mini bar yielded a split of champagne, which she poured into a flute from the shelf over the little refrigerator. Sipping it, she considered the outfit on the bed. She put the wine down and dug deeper into her suitcase, bringing out a strappy little black cocktail dress, which she lay on the bed next to the more conservative concept. She picked up her wine and took another sip, considering her options.

§

The elevator doors opened and Kat stepped off wearing the black strappy number and teetering on three-and-a-half-inch heels, a mauve shawl over her shoulders. When Jason saw her his jaw dropped for the barest second, and she immediately worried the dress was too low cut. "You look unbelievable," he said, recovering quickly. The hotel car service took them to the restaurant, the two chattering excitedly about their day the entire way. Jason told the funniest joke she'd ever heard and she laughed and laughed, touching his arm.

The restaurant was a short walk down an alley at the south end of the market, steep enough Kat had to hold Jason's arm as they descended the ancient concrete steps. The place looked like it might have been a basement storeroom at one time, converted to a warm, softly lit cave-like space, the arched supports for the building forming little alcoves for the tables. It was the most romantic restaurant space Kat had ever seen.

Jason ordered dirty martinis for them both at the bar, which they carried to their table in a quiet corner when the hostess appeared with menus under her arm.

"To team Kat," he said after they were seated, lifting his glass.

"Team Jason," said Kat, touching his glass with hers, then tasting the smoky liquid.

"You seriously never had a dirty martini?" he said.

Kat said, "First time for a lot of things today. I've never felt comfortable in meetings like that, but it felt great working with you."

"You were unbelievable," he said.

"No, you were unbelievable," said Kat as their waiter appeared.

"Will you be drinking wine?" he asked.

"Yes, we will be," said Jason, opening the wine list. He looked at Kat. "We're having fish, right, so I'm thinking a white?"

"Yes, fish," said Kat, already buzzed from her drink. "Definitely. A fat Chardonnay!"

Jason ran his finger down the Chardonnay selections. "We'll start with the ZD, 2007," he said. "I'll keep the list."

"Excellent," he said. "I'll take your order for your entrées when I bring your wine."

"Start with?" said Kat. "I'll need a helivac to get back up those stairs."

"We're celebrating," said Jason. "Today was a landmark day for MartCo, and you made it happen."

"We made it happen," said Kat, lifting her glass.

"We made it happen," he said, touching it with his, and they finished off their dirty martinis just in time for the arrival of the wine.

The waiter pulled the cork expertly and offered it to Jason, then poured a splash for his approval, which he did enthusiastically. The wine was poured and entrées ordered, grilled salmon for both, with rosemary roasted potatoes, Kat thinking how marvelous it was to be with someone who didn't have to have meat with every fucking meal, the martini having now settled comfortably into every nook and cranny of her brain.

Kat lifted her glass. "To co-working."

"To co-working," said Jason, touching his glass to hers.

"I'm so happy we were able to work out that, you know, thing. To discuss it like adults, so we could get all that, you know, out of the way and focus on the work," said Kat.

"Absolutely," said Jason, "like adults."

"Professional adults," said Kat.

§

It's hard to say who attacked whom in the hotel elevator, but their kiss lasted for twenty-three floors and their lips were still locked when they spilled out into the hallway. Kat's room was closest, and she managed to get the key card in the door in spite of him biting her neck as he cupped her breasts, pressing against her from behind.

They exploded into the room and Kat pulled him to the bed and on top of her, kissing him frantically as she removed his tie and started on the buttons on his shirt.

"Wait," said Jason, "There's something special I want you to wear."

"I can't believe you," said Kat. "We're you planning on this?"

"More like hoping," said Jason. "You're not angry, are you?"

"How could I be?" she said. "It's so romantic."

"Don't move," he said as he hurried out of the room.

So romantic, thought Kat, stretching. *How did I live without romance for so long?*

She unzipped her dress, folding it carefully, then realized what she was doing and tossed it on a chair by the bed. *No more by-the-numbers Kat.* From now on she was going to embrace life, drink fully from its cup. She considered taking off her bra and thong panties, but saw herself in the mirror over the desk with the phone and fax machine. She was wearing the only matching set she owned, pretty black lace, the bra a push-up that made her breasts swell voluptuously, and she decided to leave it on. He'd seemed very interested in her breasts.

There was a light rapping at the door. Kat opened it a crack and Jason slid in, a somewhat worn-looking brown paper Trader Joe's bag in his hand, not the packaging she was expecting.

"God, you look unbelievable," he said, dragging her to the bed, where he lavished kisses on her neck and breasts (score one for Victoria's Secret).

"So what is it you want me to wear?" she teased.

He smiled. "OK, it's a little unusual, but it really, really does it for me. Honestly? I've been imagining you in it all week."

And I thought I'd completely blown it, she thought. "Do you want me to wear it over my lingerie?"

"That would be awesome," he said as he dug into the bag, and brought out a studded black leather harness with an attached highly-detailed flesh-colored rubber penis and testicles.

§

Taylor waited in lobby, a little green around the gills, but still much improved, as rare Seattle morning sun poured in from the street and a stream of guests exited the elevator, either to check out or look for a cab. Finally the elevator doors opened and Kat appeared, wheeling her carry-on bag. Taylor's chick radar, surprisingly sensitive for a guy who owned dozens of mint Star Wars figures sealed in the original factory packaging, immediately picked up trouble.

"Are you OK?" he said as she parked her suitcase next to his.

Kat's response was delivered with a fear-inspiring intensity."Oh, just dandy. How about you?"

"I feel better. I won't go into the details, but I didn't spend the whole night in the bathroom. How was dinner?"

"Unbelievable," said Kat.

Taylor nodded sagely, wisely forgoing further interrogation. The elevator doors opened and Jason appeared, dragging his carry-on, stacked with briefcase and computer. Taylor noted Kat's rapt attention on a large Vriesea Imperialis on a nearby side table as their "team leader" passed on his way to the front desk to check them out. *Serious trouble.*

§

Taylor sat between Kat and Jason in the cab. After a lame unrequited attempt at conversation, he slept all the way to the airport and, again, took the middle seat on the flight. The only thing Kat and Jason said to one another was "excuse me," when Kat, who had the window seat, needed to use the rest room.

When they deplaned at LAX Jason said, "Well, great work guys, see you Monday."

Kat said, "Uh huh," and walked briskly away.

§

As the cab neared her street, Kat told the cabbie to turn right at the corner. Then she saw the red pickup parked in front of the Starbucks for the first time since Cooper had rescued the dove in her living room. *I wonder what adorable little surprises he has up his sleeve?* she thought, settling back into the seat. *Handcuffs? Rubber headgear with mouth balls? Golden showers?*

When the cab dropped her at her house she felt deeply satisfied to have returned to the one place in the universe that felt safe and secure and not insane. She made cookies. Three batches. She moved her book boxes to the garage. She decided to read her way through her aunt's collection, so she wouldn't sound like an idiot the next time someone asked her about a book that was actually about something that wasn't childish romantic nonsense. And she'd get a wide-screen TV and watch DVD's so the next time someone asked her if she'd seen such and such movie she could offer a thoughtful opinion. She also decided to paint the kitchen and that she was going to live in the house just fine by herself as her aunt had done.

§

The dream was back Sunday night, but now felt more real, the perspective stark. Kat could feel the breeze against her face, smell the sage, hear the murmur of the swooping crows and the whistling of their wings, and see with precise clarity the distance to the man standing at edge of the canyon watching the black pivoting birds. Her feet felt strange as she walked to where he stood and she looked down and she was barefoot. *Strange*, she thought, as if that were the only thing strange about it. She reached him and encircled him with her arms, and he turned and pressed her face against his chest, stroking her hair. *I could look up now and see his face*, she thought.

Then she remembered it was a dream, and realized someone actually was stroking her hair. She jerked awake, and there was someone standing next to her, or what seemed to be someone, as it was more of a shimmering image of a person, like a hologram. Paralyzed with fear, she fought to move, slowly raising her eyes, until she saw her aunt looking down at her.

Kat said, "Holy shit."

eleven

Not surprisingly, Kat didn't get back to sleep until six AM. When her alarm went off a half hour later, she sleepwalked the snooze button five times, the last time assuming it was the first, so found herself seriously late on a day when she seriously didn't want any trouble with Rebecca. She wasn't sure how she'd known about Jason, or even if she did, but Kat no longer felt like playing corporate politics with her boss. She also very much needed to speak with her mother. The first time, when the music box seemed to play itself, she hadn't been sure in the morning if she'd dreamt it or not. This time she'd confirmed she was awake. Something genuinely strange was going on in her new house, and she had a feeling it was in some way related to something that had happened when she was little, during that foggy period in her memory that corresponded to when her mother excised her aunt from their lives.

"Mom, pick up," Kat barked into the phone wedged on her shoulder as she filled a pastry box with cookies. "Damn it, Mother," she said, slapping the phone shut. She dropped it in her purse, taking a gulp of coffee as she checked her watch. "*Shit!*"

Kat hurried up the street, laptop and purse over her shoulder, cookie box in hand, expecting to see the bus go by at any moment. She had just stepped into low-heeled pumps, not wanting to take the time to pull on and tie her running shoes, then find a bag for the pumps, etc., but now regretted it, as they were slowing her down. She was about thirty yards from the corner when the bus passed the empty bench without stopping. Kat sprinted the remaining distance, hoping she could get the driver's attention in his mirror, but the bus was half a block away when she got to the corner. She spun around in frustration. Then, resigned, she dug in her purse for her phone to call a cab.

"Use a lift, ma'am?"

Kat looked up, surprised. It was Cooper, standing by his pickup. In her haste she hadn't seen the red truck parked in its usual spot in front of the Starbucks. She walked over to him, a little out of breath from scurrying after the bus. "I can call a cab," she said, her phone now in her hand. "I have the number speed dialed."

"How late are you?" he said.

"Late," she admitted.

Cooper raised an eyebrow. "Is that a box of those narcotic cookies?"

"Maybe."

"Go on, get in." He opened the truck's door and slid behind the wheel.

Kat climbed into the truck for the second time, and was struck again at how comfortable and familiar it felt, and also how unprincely, especially in car-conscious Los Angeles.

"Where to?" he said, turning the key and stepping on the starter button on the floor.

"Wilshire, just east of Western," said Kat, fastening the lap seatbelt, and noticing the truck's starting ritual for the first time. "The key doesn't start it?" she said.

"No," said Cooper. "Some people have them converted to a key-activated solenoid, but that reeks of heresy, you know?"

"I've always found key-activated solenoids heretical," said Kat with a solemn nod. "Although I haven't the faintest idea what that means."

"It's the thought that counts," Cooper laughed as they pulled out of the lot and entered traffic.

"Well, your truck obviously has great sentimental value," said Kat.

"Meaning why else would I be driving around in a dinosaur?"

"It is car-obsessed LA," said Kat.

"What can I say? I'm strange," said Cooper.

"How strange?" said Kat, a little too seriously.

"What do you mean?"

"Nothing. I've just had a weird week," she sighed, watching the busy city stream by.

"It's only Monday."

"Yes, it's definitely Monday," said Kat. "Anyway, I don't know how you can say you love your truck and still be driving around with that mangled fender."

"What, are you embarrassed to be seen riding in a less-than-perfect old pickup?" he said.

"Like I said, it is Los Angeles," said Kat.

"Well, if it bothers you that much, I guess I'll have to have it fixed." He stopped for a light.

"And give me the bill," she said, opening the cookie box for him.

"One of these can be a down payment," he said, making a selection. He took a bite and made a tiny moaning sound. "Chocolate chip of the Gods," he murmured.

"My version."

He took another bite. "God, what is in this?"

"If I told you I'd have to kill you."

"You already tried that."

"True. OK, my secret is these chocolate disks I get from this little Mexican grocery. Almost raw cocoa, with a whisper of cinnamon."

"'A whisper of cinnamon.' Isn't that a line from a Frost poem?" he said, his mouth only slightly full of cookie.

"There you go again, making me feel doltish with a high-brow literary reference."

"In most literary circles Frost ain't exactly high-brow," he said, putting the truck in gear as the light changed. He reached for another cookie as they lurched ahead. "Stop me if I try for a third."

"I'm sorry, but that's between you and your god," Kat said primly.

He looked at her, a little surprised. "You're a funny girl."

"Woman," she corrected.

"Sorry, 'woman.'"

"Kidding. I don't have a problem with 'girl.' And I'm flattered you think I'm funny, even if I don't read Flaubert in French."

"I'm never going to live that one down."

"No, you were right, my aunt was amazing," Kat smiled. "I sometimes feel like I'm just punching in the time clock of life, putting in my time, and then it will all be over and none of it will have meant anything."

He indicated the cookie box in her lap."Sounds like you could use one of those."

"You're right," she said, taking one.

"OK, one more," said Cooper, reaching for his third. He savored the first bite. "Wow, you need to miss the bus every day."

"No, I need to get my car back. Not driving makes something as stupid as oversleeping a few minutes a potential work-related disaster."

"What's the problem with your car? It can't have been totaled from that little scrape."

"Let's just say that this old girl is definitely packing more steel than my MINI. But you're right, my car isn't totaled, the problem is my credit card."

"That's what insurance is for."

"Yeah, but..." Kat grimaced. "They'd just finished paying for another of my mashups."

He looked at her askance. "How many have you had?"

Kat said, "Not that I don't love this subject, but how are the preparations for your show going?"

"Very well, thanks." He turned onto Wilshire. "Today's the first day I haven't had to make up for an all nighter by sleeping like a vampire. And I'm really pleased with some of the work."

"Am I still invited?"

"You are so invited," said Cooper. He leaned over, opened the glove box and removed a stack of postcards held together by a rubber band. "Here you go," he said, extracting one. "Not exactly engraved, but all the pertinent is there."

Kat read the back first, with the date and gallery information, then turned it over to find a photo of the most beautiful blown glass vase she'd ever seen. "Oh," she said. "Glass. When you said you're an artist I assumed..."

"Breaching whales and sad clowns?"

"This is wonderful," she said. "I've never seen anything quite like it. It must be amazing to get to do what you love every day."

"What you said about the time clock? My life used to be like that."

"How did you escape?"

"Well, that's the funny thing," he said. "Everyone says 'how do you get out?' I realized it's really quite simple: you just go through the door."

"That's my building," Kat said, pointing to the granite tomb she sealed herself up in Monday through Friday and the occasional night and weekend.

Cooper pulled over and stopped at the curb. He looked up at the monolithic structure, impressed. "Wow, what floor are you on?"

"The fourteenth."

"You must have quite a view," he said.

"Of beige cubicle divider and HVAC ducts. Can I ask you a weird question?" she ventured, realizing it would probably cancel out his compliment for her sparkling wit.

"OK," he said, leaning against the door and looking at her with a peculiar (for a man) attentiveness she would comment upon later to Tina.

"OK, I know this is out there, but do you believe in ghosts?"

"You mean like Casper?" he said.

"Sort of."

179

Cooper thought about this for a moment before he replied. "I've had a couple of strange experiences, things that would be hard to explain, but I have a little trouble buying the whole 'other side' thing." He chose his words carefully. "I wonder if they might be, you know, manifestations of memory."

"Like dreams?" said Kat.

"Or something we create to answer questions we aren't smart enough or brave enough to consciously ask," he said.

§

On the elevator ride to her floor Kat thought not only about how well Cooper listened, but the way he thought about the things he thought about.

"What's in the box?" Juanita said as Kat passed her cubicle.

Kat said, "I think we all know what's in the box," pausing to let her choose two (one for now, one for after lunch).

"Chocolate chip, thank you Jesus," said Juanita as she bit into her cookie.

Tina popped out of her office. "Did someone say 'chocolate chip'?"

Kat opened the box for her, thinking, *Everyone can hear everything on this floor.*

"So what happened in Seattle? Spill," said Juanita, crumbs on her blouse.

"Yeah," said Tina, "when you didn't call I figured you stayed over for a weekend of hot monkey love."

"Sadly, it was a weekend of hot monkey kitchen painting."

"Which doesn't answer my question," said Juanita. "How was the Seattle love boat? We want to hear all the juicy details."

"Trust me, you don't," said Kat, deciding to have a cookie after all.

"Are you crazy, girl?" harrumphed Juanita, "I'm a working mother of two with a husband who can't even stay awake after dinner for a NBA game on the TV. You're all I got."

"OK, let's just leave it at unbelievable."

"That more like it," said Tina.

"No, as in 'beyond belief,' a night I'll never forget, no matter how badly I want to, and I badly want to."

"Another prince bites the dust?" said Tina.

"This one didn't just bite it, he gobbled great greedy mouthfuls," said Kat. Juanita looked crestfallen. "Sorry. But you still have the Real Housewives of Hermosa Beach, or whatever coastal community they're working on now."

Tina followed her to her cubicle. "Drag. I think you really liked him."

"I kind of did," said Kat. "But I've decided I have zero ability to judge people, at least men, and the last thing I should be doing after getting out of a stifling eight year relationship is jumping into another one. I'm going to fix up my house, read some real books, learn French, do yoga, start working out, become a whole person." She remembered the card for Cooper's show. "Like this art show, this is exactly what I'm talking about." She gave Tina the card.

"It's pretty," said Tina, not sure where she was going with this.

"So you should come with me. The guy is cute too, I already told him about you."

Tina turned the card over the printed side. "Should I know who he is?"

"OK, he's the guy I hit."

"The weirdo who didn't ask for your insurance?" said Tina.

"He's not a weirdo, he's very cool, actually. A little scruffy, but cool. I mean, it's the strangest thing, he actually looks at you when you're talking to him."

"That sounds creepy," said Tina.

"Not like that, he's nice. And cute."

"It sounds like you like him," said Tina.

"I do," said Kat.

Tina looked at her. Actually, right through her. "So why aren't you going for it?"

"I like him, just not that way. Without going into it, what happened in Seattle was gross, and this after the whole Marty debacle. I'm absolutely, positively taking a break from the Prince Charming quest."

Tina looked at the card. "Tomorrow night?"

"Tomorrow night. We can get Thai food afterwards," said Kat.

Tina turned the card over and looked at the vase again. "Why not? At least you won't have to ride the bus."

"Is there something you should be doing?" said Rebecca.

Tina turned, marveling at Rebecca's stealthy approach. "I was just asking Kat for…"

"The Guiding Principles fact sheet," said Kat, opening a file folder and extracting a copy of the company protocols. "Here you go," she said, handing it Tina.

"Thanks!" gushed Tina. She indicated it to Rebecca. "I took mine home yesterday to read before bedtime and left it on my nightstand," she said before ducking into her cubicle.

Rebecca focused the warmth on Kat. "You were late again this morning."

"I missed the bus."

"Again."

"You're right, I'm sorry. I'm going to get my car fixed," said Kat.

"Probably a good idea, considering you live in Los Angeles. I'm going to have to write you up."

If Kat had been drinking something she would have done a spit take. "What?"

"I'm going to have to write you up. We're all expected here by eight AM, no exceptions."

What happened to "exemplary work"? Kat thought. She also wondered if Jason might have something to do with this. She bit her tongue, took a breath, and said. "You're right, I'm sorry. It won't happen again."

"I'm sure it won't, Kat. It's just that if I could count on anyone here it's you, and I'd like to get back to that place."

Kat felt the fury rising in her stomach. "I'm sorry, Rebecca, it won't happen again," she repeated evenly.

"Well, all right then, I'll see you at the meeting," said Rebecca, then disappeared up the desolate row of low-walled human sacrifice.

Kat looked up at the vent over her desk, whistling without a care in the world. She would just have time to pay Jason a little call before the Monday Morning Rebecca Talkfest and Timewaste, and headed for the elevators.

As she stepped off on Jason's floor she saw Meredith at the copy machine wearing black Prada pumps. *Those are actually pretty nice.* As she walked towards Jason's door the girl said, "He didn't come in today."

"OK," said Kat, hesitating.

"How was Seattle?" asked Meredith.

"Unbelievable," said Kat, noting that Meredith's thin silk top was so tight she could make out a slight roll above and below her strap, which gave her some, if meager, satisfaction.

"Should I have him call you?"

Kat thought about this for a moment, then said, "Just tell him I dropped by," and returned to the elevator, narrowly avoiding a collision with an overweight balding guy in a boxy navy Brooks Brother's suit who was distracted by Meredith's ass.

As the doors opened Kat looked back at the floating admin assistant, who nodded and smiled. Had she been invited to wield the strap-on as well? And what had Jason expected her to do with it once she was "buckled in"? Kat had kicked him out of her hotel room before he could explain. *Use it on him, I suppose.* She shuddered. *My God.*

§

That night enjoying dinner for one in her freshly painted kitchen, Kat experienced a kind of peace she'd never felt in her apartment, or for that matter anywhere else she remembered living. Falling asleep that night was easy, she was out almost as soon as her head touched the pillow. Staying asleep was more complicated. The dream was back, so familiar now it felt normal to be alone on the windy mountain ridge with a mysterious man. *At least I'm wearing clothes,* she thought, and laughed. At that moment she felt a gentle hand stroking her hair and woke, startled, and a chill ran up her back as she sensed she wasn't alone. Cautiously, she propped herself up on an elbow, and saw the ghostly image of her aunt sitting on the stool in front of the vanity. Kat said, "Aunt Ruth?" At the sound of her words the specter vanished, but not in the shimmery movie way; she was simply suddenly not there.

Kat was still awake when her alarm went off at six AM. She hadn't been so much afraid as unsettled, with sleep out of the question. Now she was so tired she considered calling in sick, then remembered the scolding she'd had from Rebecca the day before. *Such bullshit*, she thought as she dragged herself out of bed. *How many times have I been there in that death box at nine at night eating an E. coli sandwich from that stupid machine?*

She was on time, and delivered three completed project files to Rebecca, thanks to the Rebecca-free days Jason had provided the previous week. He still wasn't there. She checked. *The coward.* She was also mercilessly friendly and the very picture of by-the-book efficiency with Rebecca, including leaving precisely at five PM, right on the heels of Tina, who promised to pick her up at seven for Cooper's gallery showing.

When she exited the bus, Kat automatically looked for Cooper's truck, which, not surprisingly wasn't there; he was probably frantically preparing for his big event. She'd also started checking the little bakery with a kind of morbid curiosity. She had yet to see anyone in the place besides the snotty girl who had nearly poisoned her. Apparently it took more than an unrefrigerated case of stale Twinkies and Ho-Ho's to have a successful bakery. Go figure.

Tina was a stylish thirty minutes late picking Kat up for Cooper's show, which was OK, since it gave Kat a chance to work on the dark circles under her eyes, the result of having had practically no sleep in three days. It also allowed her to change her outfit three times. She started out with a black cocktail dress. *Doesn't really say art lover at gallery opening.* She then tried the tight white cotton blouse with skirt suit combination that had apparently fogged Jason's brain. *Too worky.* And finally settled on that same cotton blouse over tight jeans with heels. And a navy blazer. *Professional, but those tugging buttons between breasts promise a wild side.* Not that it mattered, since she wasn't shopping anyway, having practically taken a vow of chastity after the Jason debacle. Anyway, the point of the evening was to set up Cooper with Tina, right?

When Kat climbed into the little yellow Volkswagen she noted that Tina probably hadn't suffered the same outfit angst that she had; she was dressed for clubbing in a tiny silk mini halter dress that gaped just enough when she leaned forward to reveal her breasts, including a hint of nipple. *If Cooper wasn't all over that he should be declared legally dead,* Kat thought, smiling at her friend's casual audacity.

"Well, you look a little better," said Tina as she steered her car away from the curb.

Kat said, "What's that supposed to mean?" as she fastened her seatbelt.

"When you came in this morning I thought 'I see dead people.' At least you have some makeup on."

"I wear makeup to work. I mean, I don't wear whore makeup, but I wear makeup."

"Are you saying I wear whore makeup?" gasped Tina.

"I meant nothing of the kind. OK, I know I look like shit. I haven't had any sleep in, like, three days."

"Why?" said Tina.

Kat wasn't sure she wanted to tell Tina the nature of her sleep problem, given her friend's phobia about ghosts. Plus, she wasn't even sure this "ghost" was real. Kat was the first to acknowledge she had a hell of an imagination. "I don't know, probably work stress?"

"God, I know what you mean. Don't you sometimes want to tell Stuckie to go fuck herself?"

"No, actually. In fact it's never even crossed my mind. And if you want to continue having a job so you can buy cute dresses and make your car payment you might want to seriously suppress that."

"Don't worry, I know I'm not ready to retire, although sometimes I think if the right offer came along, you know? I mean it might be cool to just stay home and raise babies."

"Tina, you are a baby. And what, will you be taking them to the disco?" said Kat.

"It's a club, not a disco," said Tina. "But you're right, that would be worse."

"And once you go there, you can't just resign," said Kat. "Or at least, you're not supposed to."

"You are so right, no babies for now. So how long are we staying at this thing? I'm starving, and I checked out the reviews for this great new place that has seriously nuclear Som Tum.'"

"Which for the Haoles in the audience means?"

"Papaya salad. And catfish that's supposed to be beyond Thai hot," said Tina.

"We're going to this thing for you," said Kat.

Tina smiled. "Uh huh."

"No, seriously."

§

The gallery had valet parking, with the usual contingent of Bentleys and Ferraris parked right it front for effect, the exception being Cooper's truck, which Kat loved. She proudly indicated the truck's crumpled fender to Tina. "I did that, all by myself."

Inside was airy and high-tech, and Kat was surprised at the turnout. She and Tina stopped first at a globe that looked like the wicked queen's crystal ball in

189

Snow White. Kat could swear she could see secrets and the future staring into it.

"This is awesome," said Tina. She read the folded card on the display pillar. "Awesome price too. It's called *Future Perfect*."

"I think I know why," said Kat.

"You came," a nice voice behind them said.

Kat turned and smiled at Cooper. "I keep my promises." She did the introductions. "Cooper, Tina. Tina, Cooper."

"Nice to meet you, Tina," said Cooper, then immediately turned back to Kat. "So, what do you think?"

Kat surveyed the wonderful pieces lining the shelves of the gallery in awe. "I've never seen anything like them, they're like pure imagination. And I don't seem to be alone in my opinion. I mean, pretty good crowd."

"We got a nice write-up in the LA Times," said Cooper, "but still, there are more people here than all my other shows combined. You guys want some wine?"

Kat wanted red; Tina white.

"Coming right up," said Cooper as he headed for the reception table.

"So, what do you think?" said Kat.

"You mean him?" said Tina.

"Uh, yeah, like, the reason we came?" said Kat.

"He's cute, for an old guy," shrugged Tina.

"You scare me when you talk like that," said Kat.

"No, he's cute. I see you what meant, I mean what you said about him after you tried to murder him with your car. And he seems really nice."

"Teen, he is so nice, I mean, almost to-good-to-be-true nice. You'll see," Kat said, moving on to another piece, a bowl that looked like it had been made from a huge glass starfish. "God, can you believe this?" she said.

"Hard to believe," said Tina, looking at her thoughtfully as Cooper returned.

"Here we go, red for you, and white for you," he said, giving them their wine glasses.

"Wow, yum," said Tina, sipping her Chardonnay. "And it's even not in a plastic cup."

"Restroom?" said Kat.

"Through that curtain," said Cooper, pointing to the back of the room.

Cooper watched her walk away appreciatively, then turned to Tina, on whom this wasn't lost. "You have a nice friend."

"Contest over, she's the world's best," said Tina. "So," she continued, "this was supposed to be about setting us up, but she's actually really interested in you."

Cooper smiled, rolling with it. "That's good, because I'm actually really interested in her."

"I know," said Tina, "you guys are sickening. So, can you give her a ride home?"

"Uh, sure," he said, mildly taken aback.

"Excellent, I gotta' book." Tina downed her wine in one gulp then set the glass down next to a globular vase that looked like it contained a galaxy full of burning suns. "Just tell her I went to the disco." She turned to leave.

"Thanks, Tina, you're a pretty good friend yourself."

"Yeah, too bad the contest is over," she said over her shoulder on her way out the door.

§

"That's Tina," laughed Kat as Cooper steered his truck into nighttime Los Angeles, made shiny by a light rain. "She always says exactly what's on her mind, although this was a little over the top even for her. Tonight was fantastic. Did you sell every piece?"

"No, but it's the best show I've ever had; I feel like Cinderella leaving the ball."

"And your truck started the evening out as a pumpkin?"

"No, she was and always will be just a funky old truck."

"And, naturally, she's a she."

"Naturally."

"And 'she' has a name," Kat said goadingly.

"Lucy," said Cooper.

"As in 'I Love…'"

"Yeah, well, she's a red head, you know, and really old. Speaking of Cinderella, how are things going with Prince Charming?"

Kat looked at him, surprised. "What makes you think there was a Prince Charming? I said I was taking a break."

"Just a feeling. Something about the way you explained Cinderella to me. Hey, I'm happy to be wrong."

"No, you're right," Kat sighed, thinking that a man who listens as carefully as Cooper presented different challenges.

"And?"

"He turned out to be seriously charm-challenged," she said, looking at a sad-looking old man on a bus bench who looked like he might have been there for days.

"Sorry to hear that"

"Really?

"No, not really. I mean, I'm sorry you were disappointed, but I'm happy you're not seeing anyone anymore. I mean, assuming..."

"I'm not," she said quickly. Then she laughed. "I mean, no, I'm not." She watched the passing city, glistening like glass art. "Have you always been an artist?"

Cooper thought for a moment before he spoke, a trait Kat had noticed and realized she liked from their first meeting. "In my heart, but I had to be something I wasn't first. Business major, straight from graduate school to my very own cubicle in a hermetically sealed air-conditioned building."

"I know a lot about that one. Did you ever imagine the air vents pumping out green poison gas?" she said.

"God, all the time. Anyway, someone gave me a piece of glass art, by Josh Thomson. Do you know his work?"

"I'm a glass art newbie."

"It touched me in a kind of primal way. I bought a few more of his pieces, started reading about it, became a little obsessed. Then one day, know what? It was the air vent above my desk. I was staring at it and realized that if I stayed there I was as good as dead."

"That is so weird," said Kat, "about the vent."

"Yeah, funny, huh?" he said, turning on her street. "Thomson is here in the city. I showed up on his doorstep, offered to apprentice for free. He insisted on paying me anyway. He said 'You get what you pay for.'" They reached Kat's house. Cooper pulled into her driveway and switched off the engine. "So, here we are."

"Here we are," said Kat. "Want to come in?"

"I'd love to, but I'm seriously wrecked."

"Sure," said Kat, looking at her front door, a little embarrassed.

"No, honestly, I haven't slept in, like, three days," he said.

"I know the feeling," said Kat.

"How about dinner one night? Let me cook for you."

"That would be a first."

"Seriously? No guy has ever cooked for you?"

"Never," she said.

"Well, it will be an honor to be your first. How about Friday?"

"Friday?" said Kat, surprised at his forthrightness. "OK. So, I guess I'll need your address."

"So you can take the bus? Right. What time should I collect you?"

"Seven?"

"Anything you don't eat?" he said, piling up the points.

"Meat. I don't eat meat. Fish is OK."

"Fish it will be."

She touched his arm. "Thanks for the lift, and congratulations again on, you know, tonight." She leaned over and gave him a peck on the cheek, then opened the door and climbed down to her driveway.

He watched her cross the lawn, unlock her door, wave and go inside before Lucy's engine growled to life and they drove away.

§

Having had only a few hours sleep in the last three days, Kat should have been asleep on her feet, but she felt restless and strangely elated. So she did what any reasonable person would do, she made apple spice cookies, replaying the evening in her mind. *He really does seem different, real, down to earth, and there was something powerfully familiar about him, a kind of déjà vu.* When she was done she made herself a cup of chamomile tea as the cookies cooled, and remembered Cooper saying *All The Pretty Horses* was one of the most romantic books he'd ever read. Tea mug and cookie in hand she went to her study, *So many books*, and slid Ruth's hard-bound copy from the shelf. She read almost to the end of the second page, then took it and her tea (and another cookie) to the bedroom and started over, determined to get it. And soon she did, reading for two hours before she fell asleep, entranced by the poetry and song of McCarthy's prose.

Kat started awake at midnight, feeling groggy and weird. Dropping her clothes and her bra on the way to the bathroom, she leaned against the sink in her panties and brushed her teeth, thinking about horsemen in the Mexican badlands. Returning to bed, she slept dreamlessly for about three hours, until she found herself on the windswept mountain of her dream again, but alone; the familiar figure, the man whose face she'd never been able to see, was gone.

Suddenly panicked, she felt the most intense sense of loss she'd ever experienced, then stopped and laughed to herself. *I haven't even seen his face, and anyway I'm dreaming.* Then she heard the sound of cantering hooves and turned just as a lone rider swept her up onto the back of his horse and pulled her arms around his chest as they rode into the wind. Even though she couldn't see his face she knew it was the same man who had been haunting her dream, and she rested her head against his shoulder. He reached back to stroke her hair, and when she felt his hand she woke to see the now familiar figure of her aunt beside the bed, looking down at her with serious eyes. Kat said, "Aunt Ruth, what is it? Please tell me, I've got to get some sleep," but the specter vanished.

Perhaps she was getting used to living with a real live (dead?) ghost, but Kat fell back to sleep immediately, mumbling, "Maybe she wants a martini," to no one in particular, and actually woke feeling refreshed and ready for whatever the day would bring. She walked up to the bus stop early so she could get a Starbuck's latté. The coffee shop was jammed and as she waited to order she saw the little bakery at the other end of the parking lot wasn't open. When she'd been served, she walked across the lot to the deserted shop and looked in the window, sipping her coffee and nibbling on an apple spice cookie from the box she'd brought for her coworkers. The little all-stainless kitchen, with its commercial ovens, Hobart mixer, counters, sink and racks was a baker's porn.

Of course Kat stopped at security in the lobby of her building so Gus could choose a cookie. Two women followed her onto the elevator, one of whom commented on the scents wafting from the pastry box in her hand. She opened it and they each chose one, making suitable moaning noises as they bit into their treats.

"Where did you get these?" one of them asked.

"A place in my neighborhood," said Kat as she got off at her floor.

"Morning," Kat said as she passed Juanita's cubicle, making no attempt to hide the pastry box. She put it on her desk, along with her laptop and purse and sat down to boot up her computer. Waiting, she leaned back in her chair and considered the whistling air vent of death.

Juanita suddenly appeared in the doorway. "What have we here?"

"Good morning to you too. Help yourself."

Juanita opened the box and her face registered an almost religious awe. "Apple spice?"

"Apple spice," said Kat.

"Bless my soul," said Juanita as she carefully separated one from its fellows. She closed her eyes as she bit into it. "Goodness," she said simply, and finished it off in a most unladylike manner.

"Don't stop now," said Kat.

"OK," said Juanita, helping herself to a another.

"Can I ask you something?" said Kat.

"I hope so," said Juanita.

"Have you ever had the exact right person say the exact right thing to you at the exact right moment of your life? Last night I had an epiphany."

"Something you can take for that?" said Juanita, nearly done with her second cookie.

"No, I mean…"

"I know what it means," interrupted Juanita. "Girl, you're not starting on another prince, are you?"

"No, of course not. I just met somebody nice, like, you know, a new friend."

"Uh huh," said Juanita. "So, you have plans Sunday? Boo's breaking in his new grill. Thing's big as a damn car."

"Sure, it'll be fun to see the girls," said Kat. "OK if I bring someone?"

"This new 'friend'?"

"Maybe," said Kat.

§

The rest of the week went well. Kat decided that she was going to inform Jason in no uncertain terms that she would expect a dazzling review of her work on the Seattle project, and that would be that. They would be polite and professional when they encountered each other in the business environment, otherwise she never wanted to speak to him again. But when she tried again to see him, Miss T & A told her he was taking some vacation days, which was just as well, since she was in a really good mood and that conversation was going to be a serious buzz kill. Rebecca, whom Kat never underestimated, clearly had a pretty good idea of how angry she was and had reverted to her good cop disguise, supportive and encouraging. Kat, in turn, practically shouted "Sir! Yes Sir!" in reply to anything Rebecca said to her, and they circled each other like a pair of wary cats.

twelve

...She moved through the lingering shadows thrown by the moonlight pouring from the nightblack sky, her white cotton skirt whipping at the ankles above her bare feet. When she reached the stable she looked back again to be sure she wasn't followed, as she had repeatedly since she'd left her room and stepped silently out of the house into the dark warm summer night. Sure no one was there, she cracked the door enough to see where he slept on the cot in the corner behind the saddles and beneath the tack, wincing at the groan of the hinges on the huge rough wooden doors. Slipping inside, she moved through the darkness, surefooted from a short lifetime of work and play amongst the horses who now shifted in their stalls, the most alert among them nickering softly at the sound of her calloused feet and the smell of her.

Reaching him, she knelt, sensing his heat and scent, then bent over as if to kiss him, which she'd imagined only in her most private longings when she teased herself with thoughts of the warmth and firmness of his lips and the weight of his body on her own. Her tousled hair played on his face and he woke violently, his hand closing on her neck. She neither resisted nor withdrew.

It's me, she whispered.

I know that now, durn' fool. I'm not a good one to be creepin' up on.

I like your hand there, she said, and he put his hand back on her throat, but gently.

This is crazy, you know, he said, his hand now finding her face. Last person your people want to see you with is a Gringo without a centavo.

You should care what I think, not my people.

Tell me what you want me to do; I'll do anything you say. There was a kind of hopelessness in his voice she liked.

I want to go where the wind is cool and we can talk like a woman and a man. She took his hand to make him stand up, but he said, Wait and turn around for God's sake, and she did, smiling to herself. They led their horses out, her huge shiny black stallion and the little North American sorrel mare with her big rump he called Lucy, which she loved the sound of. The black and the red.

Then they pulled themselves on, and rode silently out, side by side, bareback, quieter than the cicadas that purred in the trees about the hot night.

At the mountain's foot they broke into a gentle canter, side by side, knees brushing, up past the brush and scrub oak till they reached the treeline of pine and birch brushed by a cool breeze that kissed her face and she kicked the stallion into a run, impatient for the clear water beneath the falls. When he reached her the stallion was chest deep, drinking, as she lay on his neck and the man slid off the mare and rubbed her glistening neck and threw the reins over so she could drink too. He pulled his boots off and his shirt and waded in, splashing his face, then floated onto his back, his eyes full of the moon now full and tall in the black sky freckled with a million tiny flaming suns. Then he felt her beside him and he righted himself. He saw the whiteness of her skirt and blouse draped on the stallion, then felt her hands on his shoulders, pulling herself to him to keep her head above the water, and his hands slipped down the smoothness of her naked back.

Catalina, he whispered.

We can speak here," she said in a public tone of voice.

Catalina, he repeated, loud enough that Lucy looked up from her long drink and snorted jealously.

203

Me quieres? she said, softly now.

"Yo, mama, I so love you," he said, his voice jarringly childish and nasty...

The kid, on his knees in the seat in front of Kat, grinned back at her as his friends standing in the aisle cracked up. Leaning over the back of the seat now he said, "How 'bout I lose my friends here and we go someplace I can get you pregnant?"

Kat, now a grizzled veteran of Los Angeles public transportation, regarded him coolly. He looked about twelve, for God's sake, and he and the bros in his posse were carrying backpacks overflowing with text books. One of them had an Apple laptop satchel, further diminishing their street cred.

Kat saw they were approaching her stop. "Thanks," she said, getting to her feet, "but when I'm ready for a baby daddy, he's going to have to at least be in high school." At this the kid's friends roared, teasing and punching him as she moved down the aisle, smiling to herself.

She was still smiling when she stepped down to the curb, not only from her little victory on the bus, but because she felt like something special was going to happen that night. Cooper really did seem different than any man she'd ever met. When she'd been with him she'd felt anything was possible. *So much for my hiatus from princes.* She glanced at the little bakery as she passed the mall, empty as usual, except for the lone girl. *They should call the place Twinkies & Rudeness*, she thought.

She walked in her door precisely at six and loved the strangeness of not having to rush to get ready for her dinner date as she would have if she'd left work at the previously normal late hour, thinking, *Rebecca actually did me a favor*. Five outfit changes later, her time cushion evaporating, she settled on a version of what she'd worn to the gallery. Jeans just felt like, well, Cooper. Tight, designer, sexy of course, but still jeans. She only had to interview four pairs of shoes before deciding on some serious heels that she was pretty sure made her ass look great, or at least as good as it was going to look until she lost the five pounds she'd decided that morning she was going to lose. And she'd bought a blouse when she'd gone out for lunch (thanks again, Rebecca), another tight crisp cotton blouse, orange (like everything in the magazines now), whose buttons pulled nicely between her breasts (why mess with success?). She heard Cooper's truck in her driveway almost precisely at seven.

§

Kat pulled the shoulder belt over and fastened it as they drove up her street towards Olympic. "I'm surprised Lucy even came with seatbelts, let alone this kind," said Kat.

"You're right, they didn't have any belts in those days. Purists in the old truck world seriously frown on these. Fortunately I don't live in old truck world. I did keep the floor starter button, but mostly because it works and I figure it might confuse potential thieves."

"Is Lucy a hot commodity?"

"I get several offers a week; I couldn't believe it when somebody told me what she's worth. I've had her for over fifteen years; she was my father's. I put her in storage while I was in school, then had her restored with the first money I made. My will states they have to dig a hole big enough for both of us."

"You both look like you have plenty of miles left on you," smiled Kat.

"Thanks. You're a fine healthy thing yourself." said Cooper.

"Thank you," said Kat, feeling all of the above.

"So are you moved in?" said Cooper.

"I am. Even painted my kitchen, and I've started sorting my books."

"Are they fighting it out with your aunt's, or did you get more shelves?"

"It wasn't much of a fight, as you noticed."

"I did no such thing."

"I saw you judging my books. And it's not fair, since I seriously doubt you've ever actually read one, I mean a Romance novel."

He said, "Mea culpa, mea maxima culpa."

"Thank you. I left a few out, but the rest went to the garage. I've read most of them several times anyway." Cooper looked at her sideways. "There you go again," she said.

"Sorry. Tell you what, pick one out, pick out the best one of the lot and I'll read it," he said.

"No you won't. It's OK, I enjoy them, it's enough. But you inspired me in a way."

"I love hearing that," he said.

"I thought you would," said Kat. "Anyway, I want to read what my aunt read. I want to understand and know who she was. And, OK, I started with the Romance book you recommended."

"The Romance book?"

"*All The Pretty Horses*."

"I said it was romantic, I doubt McCarthy would like hearing it described as Romance."

"In other words it doesn't have a happy ending?" said Kat.

"How far are you into it?" he said.

"Far enough I'm counting the pages because I don't want it to end."

"I did the same. I just found it so beautiful, like word jazz," he said.

"You didn't answer my question," she said.

"And I have no intention of doing so," said Cooper as he steered his truck up the onramp onto the 405 freeway.

"I thought you lived in the neighborhood," said Kat. "I mean seeing you, you know, at the Starbucks all the time."

"It's not that far, but I live more on the West Side," said Cooper. "When I take a coffee break from work I like to drive a little to clear my head. I decided to try every Starbucks in LA. I thought it would be a good way to, I don't know, take the pulse of different neighborhoods. Feel the vibe."

"So how come I kept seeing you at that one?"

Cooper smiled, thinking about this before he spoke. "Because I wanted to talk to you again."

"Really," said Kat, surprised.

"Really," said Cooper.

§

"Sixty-hour weeks, plus nights and weekends, and she's writing me up?" said Kat, sitting on a barstool in Cooper's kitchen holding a glass of Chardonnay, while one of her pumps dangled from a toe. "I mean, I'm doing my work, plus everybody else's. Tina, bless her soul, gets migraines, translation: hangovers. I've been finishing her projects and taking my work home. I'm just so friggin' agreeable."

"That's what I can't stand about you," said Cooper, mincing herbs with a huge Hitchcock-worthy chef's knife.

"You know what I mean," said Kat.

"The agreeable shall inherit the earth," he said, scooping the results of his chopping into a bowl.

"If there's any of us left standing," she said.

"We'll still be standing—we're strong, we're resilient, we're determined." He lifted his glass in a toast, "The Few; The Proud; The Agreeable."

"To The Agreeable," agreed Kat, lifting her glass. She finished her wine and held her glass out. "In the words of a famous glass artist I know, please sir, may I have a little more?" Cooper refilled it, then topped up his own, taking a sip before returning to his prep, and Kat watched him work, noting his focus, which she found adorable, another dimension to an already overflowingly multi-dimensional man.

The kitchen wall had been opened to the living room, which was populated with beautiful wood and leather furniture, two dramatic glass vases of likely heritage, and an eight-foot high grandfather clock with a smiling moon above its face.

"Your house is just to die for," said Kat. "I love the rustic antique-y thing with the ultra-modern kitchen. Is that sofa Ralph Lauren?"

"No, it's the real thing; it was my parents'. I grew up with nearly all this furniture."

"It looks new."

"They took care of it, and so have I."

"You said you inherited Lucy fifteen years ago. They must have been young."

"Yes, they were."

"If it's weird, I mean…"

"No, it's OK. I feel more angry and cheated than tragic. Car accident, although when the other driver is blind drunk they upgrade it from 'accident' to manslaughter, especially if it's happened, like, six fucking times before." Cooper caught himself. "Sorry, like I said, more angry than tragic."

"It's OK, there are times when 'friggin' doesn't cut it."

"I've never been able to say that word," he said. "The Austin Powers movie was the last straw."

"I saw that one! There, I'm not totally uncultured."

The grandfather clock struck the hour, the bell sounding eight times. "Exactly on time," said Kat, checking her watch.

"I know, it's amazing; it's over a hundred and fifty years old," said Cooper. "It was a wedding gift from my great-grandfather to my great-grandmother."

"So much of your family seems to be a part of you. Do you have siblings?"

"Only child. My mother used to say nothing could happen to me 'cause they didn't have a backup kid. So she goes and, well, you know."

"I wish I could have met them."

"They were very solid folk. They would have liked you."

Kat got down from the stool and leaned on the counter. "So, what's on the menu?"

"I call it Simple Salmon, fillets sautéed in olive oil and butter, seasoned only with a few herbs and S and P."

"S and P?"

"Salt and pepper." He sandwiched the salmon fillets between sheets of wax paper, then pounded them with a small, heavy saucepot.

"Why are you punishing that poor fish?"

"So it cooks quickly and evenly."

"Very impressive."

"That's the other reason. As for the rest of the evening's fare, we'll also be enjoying rosemary roasted fingerling potatoes and spinach sautéed with a whisper of garlic."

"No need to whisper, I love garlic."

"An important quality in this house," he said, as he opened the oven door on the huge stainless-steel Wolf range to check on the potatoes.

"I'm suffering serious stove envy. Make that serious kitchen envy," said Kat.

"That old girl you have can do anything this jet fighter can do, with less gas and fuss, long as it isn't too big." He turned on one of the oversized burners on his "jet fighter."

"My God," said Kat.

"Yeah, they're, like, fifteen-thousand BTU's," he laughed as he slid an oiled sauté pan onto the flame.

"So, I thought there'd be glass art everywhere."

"Well, you know, if a piece works…"

"You sell it."

"Gotta' pay the rent," he said, watching the pan heat up. "And if it doesn't, I recycle it until it does."

"Have you ever had a piece that was so perfect you couldn't part with it?"

"In fact, I did. Melted it down on the spot. You have to be careful with perfection, the gods are insanely jealous."

"Anyone ever say you have a sexy brain?" she smiled.

"Uh, not to my face," he said. "I have a few new pieces in my workshop, something new I've been working on. I'll take you out there later."

"I'd love that."

The pan started to smoke and he plopped in the fish and dusted it with herbs. Kat was silent, a little awed at his concentration, until he flipped the fillets, added more herbs and poured a cup of white wine into the pan, which exploded in flames. She gave him a standing ovation.

"Thank you," Cooper said, bowing graciously.

And Kat thought, *It can be like our dreams.*

A half of another bottle of wine and butter lettuce with a champagne vinaigrette and medium rare Salmon fillets and roasted potatoes and garlicky spinach sauté drizzled with lemon and coffee granita with triple-chocolate biscotti later, the latter served with decaf espresso, Kat sat back in her chair a very satisfied feline. "God, that was incredible."

212

"Thanks. Cooking for someone is a primal pleasure, isn't it? One of our most basic connections. Tasting one of your cookies taught me worlds about you."

"Watching you cook, and eating the results did the same for me," said Kat, "but I'm greedy for more. Is Mr. Science ready to take me on a tour of his la*bor*atory?"

"That would be <u>Doctor</u> Science, and, yes, the official post-prandial tour is about to begin. Walk this way," he said, dragging a foot Igor-style toward the kitchen door, the corny joke making Kat feel somewhat better for the silly things she'd probably said in the course of the evening. She followed him out to a backyard dominated by a huge willow tree, beneath which was a small guest house, like a fairytale cottage nestled in the woods. He opened the unlocked door and switched on the light, and Kat stepped into his world.

The workshop was messy in a well-used sort of way, but orderly, with the tools that weren't on the worktables or benches hung neatly on the walls. There were also gas canisters and blowtorches, but the main attraction was a black iron furnace, which fascinated her.

"That's the crucible, a little sun of focused heat," said Cooper.

Kat considered a vase on one work bench that looked like a swirling fountain of fire. "It's so beautiful," she said, emotions fortified by the wine and dinner. "Like something you dreamed."

"That's exactly where I first saw it. I woke up at, like, five this morning and I could still see it so clearly. What's been great about developing the craft is that I'm more and more able to translate what I imagine into, as you say, something real."

"I hope it isn't perfect, I don't want you to melt it down just so some stupid god doesn't get his feelings hurt."

"No worries," laughed Cooper, "it still has plenty of flaws." Entranced by the vase, Kat didn't see him opening a cabinet door behind her. "There's something else I've been working on that you might find interesting," he said. She turned and he held a life-sized glass slipper in his hands.

Rarely at a loss for words, Kat was at a loss for words.

"You said there weren't any. I thought that was sad, and there should be." He gave it to her and she turned it over in her hands, awed.

"I wasn't sure about the fit," he said.

"It couldn't be more perfect." She put her hand behind his head and pulled his lips to hers and, while it wasn't the hottest kiss two lovers ever shared in the history of the world, it was one of the softest and sweetest. "Take me to your bed," she said, their lips barely touching, then added, "I've always wanted to say that." He kissed her again, then took her hand, her precious slipper clutched tightly to her breast and led her back to his house, through a yard lashed by a hot wind that seem to have magically appeared.

"It's a Santa Ana," said Cooper. He put his arm over her shoulders and they ducked their heads into it as Kat's hair whipped across her face and tiny cyclones of leaves danced around them.

"Where did it come from?" asked Kat as he led her to the house.

"From the wind place."

Inside, the house was dark. Cooper tried several light switches. "I'll check the breakers, but I have a feeling a line is down from the wind," he said.

"Don't," she said, putting a hand on his arm.

He smiled. "You're right, this is definitely a candle moment," and together they found the bedroom in the semi-darkness where his huge sleigh bed was soon surrounded by dozens of shimmering votive lights, several of which illuminated a glass slipper nestled safely atop a bureau among framed photos of Cooper's parents and small imperfect glass art experiments. And in that gentle light they undressed each other for the first time, and their delight was like opening their presents on Christmas morning and the love they made was the promise Kat had known was there in her heart. And the promise was this man.

Afterwards they fell asleep, making the spoons, Cooper's arm under her head, and they slept more deeply and peacefully than either of them had for weeks and months and years. Kat stirred just before midnight as the last of the votive lights was flickering out, and Cooper woke too and nuzzled her neck.

"So many candles," she said, smiling at the feel of his chest on her back.

"Hey, I'm competing with Barbara Cartland," he said.

"You're not competing with anyone."

He shook his hand. "Is it asleep?" she said as she moved to free it.

"It's OK," he said, pulling her back. "It's worth it." And she settled blissfully back on his arm. "I read this article about a sleep study these doctors were doing. They noticed this interesting syndrome—several of the men were suffering numbness in one arm, just one. Turns out they were newlyweds." He kissed her on the back between the shoulder blades. "The sad thing was it generally went away after the first year."

"Generally?"

"Not always."

Kat snuggled in as the grandfather clock chimed, once, twice, ten times more, and precisely at the moment of the twelfth chime a door slammed somewhere in the house.

"What was that?" she said, not terribly worried.

Cooper, very worried, said, "Shit," and was barely out of bed when the bedroom door flew open, crashing against the wall, and a beautiful blond woman, wild-haired and barefoot, wearing what appeared to be green cotton scrubs, exploded into the room screaming, "What the fuck is this?"

"Who is she?" said Kat, cowering under the covers.

"Who am I? Who the fuck are you, and what are you doing in bed with my husband?" shrieked the harridan.

"Get out, Sally. Wait in the living room; I'll be there in a minute," said Cooper.

"The fuck I will!" screamed the woman, tearing the bedclothes out of the terrified Kat's desperate grasp. Then she fell on Kat, slapping her and tearing at her hair. Cooper leaped over the bed and pulled the mad woman off of his terrified lover, who leaped out of bed, grabbing her clothes and shoes and purse on the way to the door.

"Kat, wait!" he called after her, but she'd already reached the living room, pulling her clothes on along the way. She ran out the front door, carrying her shoes and didn't look back, so she didn't see Cooper standing naked in the doorway, watching her running up the sidewalk, barefoot, as the woman continued to rage behind him.

§

Kat didn't put her shoes on until she'd reached a bus bench a safe ten blocks away. And only then did she grant herself the luxury of crying, which began with

217

a huge heaved sob, followed by a torrent of tears. She looked in her purse for a tissue. Of course she didn't have one. She looked around, trying to get her bearings. Would a bus from here take her anywhere near her house? Were there even any buses running this late? *So stupid*, she thought, pulling out her phone to call a cab. *Everything you do is stupid. Stupid, stupid, stupid. Stupid men,* she thought, dialing, *stupid books, stupid thoughts. What was I thinking? I don't even know that person I just went to effin' bed with. No, fucking bed with. It was definitely a fucking bed.*

"City Cab, please hold," said a detached voice on her phone.

Kat sighed, holding it to her ear. *Stupid, stupid, stupid.* Then she saw a bus approaching several blocks away and ended the call. *Or maybe it's a ghost bus,* she thought, laughing through her tears. *I'm about to get on a ghost bus to nowhere in the middle of fucking Los Angeles.*

The bus covered the blocks quickly with no other passengers waiting on its route, and stopped at her bench. The double doors opened and the driver looked down at her. Kat looked up at him, surprised he was real.

"You want to get on?" he said.

Kat got to her feet and stepped up to him, then realized it costs money. Not so much sobbing now as whimpering, cheeks streaked with teary mascara, she dug through her purse for change as the driver closed the doors behind her. "It's OK lady, just sit down," he said putting the bus into gear.

Kat mumbled, "Thanks" as she stumbled to a nearby seat, where she pressed herself against the window and started to cry again for real. A moment later a reassuring voice said, "*Aqui tienes, mi'ja*," and she turned to see an older Latina with a gentle smile offering her a handful of tissues.

· *thirteen*

Kat, wearing Ray Bans, a tank top, cut-off jeans and sandals, sat on a bench at the picnic table in Juanita's back yard, neatly peeling and shredding the label from her beer. Her phone rang, and she pulled it out of her purse, checked the caller ID and promptly dropped it back in her bag.

"Him?" said Tina, sitting across from her wearing huge sunglasses, a little cotton sundress and stacked espadrilles.

"Again. Can you believe it?" She took the last sip from her beer. "He has some nerve. Can you believe it? I mean, he hadn't said a word about her. Can you believe it?"

"I believe it," said Tina.

"What would you call someone like that? What kind of person would do something like that?"

"A guy?"

"Yeah, a guy," said Kat as she got up to get another beer from the cooler on the grass beside the Hummer-sized stainless steel grill.

Boo, wearing a "Kiss the cook!" apron and Dr. Dre headphones, the latter blasting a baseball game, lifted one headphone and indicated a green-spotted patty in the corner of the grill, well clear of the juicy hamburgers and sizzling hot dogs.

"Sad looking little thing," he said. "What exactly is in that?"

"Dried vegetable matter and gritty little bits of soy."

"Don't seem natural."

"Natural is the point," she said, twisting the cap from the perspiring bottle. She sat back down across from Tina and selected a potato chip large enough she had to break it to fit in her mouth.

"I like my burgers bloody," Tina said.

"It gonna' moo at you," Boo assured her as he replaced his headphone, returning to the game.

Tina watched Kat obsessively shredding the label on her beer. "So, are you OK?"

"Define OK."

"Uh, not insane?"

"Maybe Marty's right. Maybe I need to stop living in Katland. Come back to earth. Face reality."

"Rotate your tires. Brush three times a day. Eat more fiber," Tina added helpfully.

Juanita came out of the house carrying two huge bowls, one filled with slaw, the other potato salad. "You OK, honey?" she said to Kat, as she sat down next to Tina and put the bowls on the table.

"I'm OK," said Kat, getting a little annoyed, even though she knew her friends meant well. "I'll certainly live."

"Damn straight you will," said Juanita as she ladled herself a hefty glass of sangria. "You're smart and beautiful and successful and sweet and strong, and you're gonna' be just fine."

"Well, since you put it that way," said Kat. "How many guys did you date before you met Boo?"

"Didn't date any; Mama wouldn't allow it. I had to join the Army to even talk to one, and we talked for a year before we had one smooch, 'cause Mama swore all men are dogs after only one thing, and it's your job to make sure they don't get it." At that moment five-year-old Sasha, wielding a Super Soaker, blasted out of the house chasing the squealing Patrice, who was four.

"Apparently you fell down on the job," said Tina, indicating the shrieking girls. "And I'm guessing backwards."

"You are bad," Juanita giggled. "Also correct." She looked at her daughters running around the grill and her husband, oblivious thanks to his noise-canceling baseball game. "I did, and I don't regret that for one minute, but I also don't regret not getting to experience what you two are going through. My mama was a bitter

222

woman, probably because my daddy, well, I never even met the man. But wisdom is paying attention. She used to play this record all the time, 'If you make it with a stranger, you sure better know the score, 'cause no matter what he tells you, there's bound to be a whole lot more." She indicated her daughters. "When they get to that age, my advice to them going to be 'Slow the heck down.'"

"Amen to that," said Kat.

Sasha reversed course and Patrice didn't stop in time to avoid a huge blast from the squirt gun, soaking her T-shirt. "Stop it!" she howled, "my titties are getting wet."

"You don't have any titties, baby," said Juanita.

"They'll grow if I water them!" squealed Sasha, unleashing another blast from the gun.

"Put that dam thing away!" barked Juanita, every bit the master sergeant herself.

"But…" started Sasha.

"No buts but your little one getting in the house to put your sister in a dry T-shirt."

Sasha heaved a dramatic sigh and hung her head, then took her sister's hand and led her toward the house. As they passed their mother, Juanita said, "Give me that," tearing the squirt gun from her hand and tossing it on the table.

"God they're cute," Kat said, watching them go into the house.

"Cute only goes so far when a water pistol's involved," said Juanita.

"More like a cannon," said Tina.

"His brilliant idea," said Juanita, indicating Boo. "Then he puts those things on his ears so he doesn't have to listen to them fight over it."

"He probably just wanted to play with it himself," said Kat.

"That's the Lord's truth," said Juanita. Never met a man who was mentally older than twelve." She looked at Boo, harvesting the meat (and Kat's bark burger) from the grill. "Still a day doesn't pass I don't thank the good Lord for my lover man."

Boo took his headphones off, picked up the platter and turned around to find the three women smiling at him.

"What?" he said.

"Nothing, Lover Man," said Tina.

"That about right," Boo said, sitting down and putting the platter on the table. "Now gimme' those plates—daddy makes a mean burger, and his dogs ain't too shabby neither."

The girls came out of the house, Patrice in a dry shirt. "Did you wash those hands?" said Juanita.

"Yes, ma'am," said Sasha, starting to sit down.

"Let me see 'em," said Juanita, and they dutifully held them out. "There's enough dirt under those nails to plant potatoes," she clucked. "Sit down and pass your plates."

Boo looked at Kat. "So you want I go over there and break that boy's legs?"

Juanita slapped his arm. "Lord, man, she doesn't want you to know about that."

"I was just sayin'."

"It's OK," said Kat, "no reason everybody shouldn't know what a loser I am."

"Oh, honey," said Juanita, her consolation interrupted when Patrice stuck her tongue out at her sister and Sasha grabbed it in her fist. Patrice howled and swung at her, knocking over her glass of cranberry juice which flooded the table, causing the adults to leap to their feet. Patrice leaned against her mother, sniffling tears as Juanita mopped up the mess with napkins. Crisis over, everyone sat back down.

"Crybaby," sneered Sasha at her sister.

"You are one more remark like that from spending the rest of the day in your room," said Juanita as she passed Boo the potato salad. He piled his plate, then started shoveling salad in on top of a huge mouthful of burger. Juanita looked at Kat, indicating her husband with a nod as she spoke. "You know those pretty stories you're always reading? This is what happens after the prince rescues you."

"The rescue isn't all it's cracked up to be either," said Kat.

§

A veggieburger, potato chips and salad, corn, cake and five beers later, Kat waited outside the powder room to pee, listening to the fascinating murmur of the two little girls. "Are you guys almost done in there?" she asked through the door, and two little voices answered in the affirmative. Finally it opened and Sasha came out, followed by Patrice, who was focused on fastening her jeans.

"What were you guys doing in there?" said Kat.

Sasha shrugged, "I was teaching Patrice how to poo."

"Doesn't she already know how to do that?"

"Yeah, in her pants. I was showin' her how to do it in the toilet like a big kid."

"Like a big kid like you."

"Yeah."

"You're a good sister."

"I know," said Sasha as she headed for the yard, followed by Patrice, who shadowed her sister's every move, even if it did frequently lead to mayhem and torture.

Kat went into the bathroom, turned on the light, closed the door, and looked at the toilet.

"Oh, dear."

fourteen

Cooper called Kat four more times over the weekend, the last Sunday evening around eight. In each case she saw his caller ID and didn't answer, and in each case he left no message, and if he had she would have simply deleted it. There was nothing the man could say to her at this point that would justify having sex with her in the bed he shared with his wife, much less doing that without even telling her he was married.

Exhausted from over two days of crying, she fell asleep effortlessly and dreamlessly, until what had become a familiar witching hour in her new home, three AM. She was back on the ridge, the wind whipping her face. The familiar figure was at the rim of the canyon, and still very much a mystery (he couldn't be Cooper). But there was something new, a light golden haze, as if she were looking through a filter, making her acutely aware she was more an observer than a participant in her dream. Then she turned to see a lovely woman in her forties walking noiselessly toward the man. She passed closely enough that Kat could have reached out and touched her. Apparently the woman couldn't see her, although she stopped for a moment and looked back, as if aware someone might be there, and it was at that moment that Kat realized it was Ruth. But not the old woman who had left Kat her home and library, it was the aunt who had been her eight-year-old niece's best friend. Ruth continued walking towards the man without making a sound, her long skirt tearing at the brush. When she reached him she put her hand on his shoulder and he looked around at her and smiled, then took her into his arms, combed the hair from her face with his fingers and kissed her fully and deeply on the mouth, a kiss which Ruth returned with all her body and soul.

And like a bolt from the blue Kat knew who he was, and while aware she was dreaming, that the kiss was very real, and with that revelation the scene changed to the street in front of her house, except, oddly, she was riding the bicycle she'd gotten for Christmas when she was eight and she realized she was on the sidewalk on the opposite side of the street and, suddenly afraid, stopped behind a huge tree thinking, *This tree isn't here now.* She looked across the street, and everything about the house seemed normal, except the lawn was green and manicured and she saw the too familiar Ford LTD parked in the driveway. She

228

suddenly only wanted to turn and ride away as fast she could, but she was paralyzed, frozen in the dream as she now realized she had been that day, because what she was watching actually happened, and now she was seeing it again.

The door opened and the man from the mountain came out, and she shook, wanting to cry out and run, but she was frozen like an insect in amber. The man was followed by the Ruth from her dream, the Ruth who had been her best friend and played makeup with her and baked with her and read her marvelous stories. They seemed upset and Kat pressed herself against the tree so they would never know she'd been there, could never know that she'd seen. He started down the stairs from the porch, but Ruth grabbed his sleeve and pulled him back and into her kiss, the same kiss from the mountain.

Kat woke with the same feeling of fear and confusion and nausea she'd felt in her dream. Even though she hadn't seen him in twenty-two years and her mother had destroyed every trace of him in their lives, she was sure the man was her father. And, though the air in her bedroom was still and empty, she knew she wasn't alone.

§

After the dream, Kat had tossed and turned, finally falling back to sleep at five, and slept through her alarm. Walking up the aisle of cubicles, with their beige fabric-covered walls, she dreaded the inevitable conversation, Stuckey's stern schoolmarm scolding the tardy child. *Which I might as well be*, she thought. She'd tried to reach her mother again, calling at eight, knowing Jean had been up for at least an hour, and of course got no answer. *That's how we deal with things we don't want to deal with*, thought Kat, *we just will them away.*

Juanita wasn't at her desk. Neither was Tina, but someone else was, a twenty-something guy with stylish horn-rimmed glasses and a blue oxford shirt and gold tie over chinos and boat shoes. The full Polo. Kat stopped and stared at him.

"Good morning," he ventured with a tentative smile.

"Who are you?" she said, definitely not smiling.

"Uh, Todd," he said. "Todd Smiley?"

"What are you doing here?"

"I'm, like, a temp?"

"Where's Ms. Prem?"

"I don't know her. But there was some stuff left in a few of the drawers." He picked up an inbox with a Hello Kitty keychain, a pack of tissues, a tortoise hair clip, sunglasses case and a pink birth control dispenser. "Maybe you could give it to her?"

Kat looked at the box in his hand, then hung her laptop over her shoulder and took it to her own little space, where she dropped it, her purse and computer on her desk and threw herself into her chair. She thought for a moment, then dug her phone out of her purse and speed-dialed Tina, muttering "A temp!" to herself as it rang through to her friend's voicemail.

"This is Teen," the message began, "let's party!"

Stupidest message I've ever heard, thought Kat as she waited for the beep, after which she said, "It's me. What the hell is going on? Call me, like now?"

She threw the phone on her desk and booted up her computer, but was out of her chair before the Windows greeting had sounded.

§

Rebecca was having a bad day too. In addition to firing Tina Prem, which she hadn't enjoyed as much as she'd thought she would because she wasn't actually nearly as cold and tough as she pretended to be, *her* boss was on her ass about the same thing he was always on about, The Numbers, which she'd decided would never be adequate, since every new plan had a new The Numbers. Her door had been ajar when the call came and normally she would have excused herself for a moment to close it, but he'd been in such a lather she hadn't been able to get a word in, which was why she hadn't been able to simply ignore Kat's firm knock. "I'm not sure we have the resources now to realize that goal," she said into the phone as she held a palm up to Kat, trying to indicate she couldn't talk.

Undeterred, Kat said, "What the hell is going on?"

Rebecca held a "just a minute" finger in the air.

"No. No more fingers in the air," said Kat. "I need to talk to you now."

Rebecca sighed. "I have someone here and it looks like an emergency. I'll call you back as soon as I've dealt with it," she said into the phone and hung up. She sat back in her chair and fixed Kat with her steeliest glare. "Coincidently, that was *my* boss I just cut short. What's on your mind?"

"Where's Tina?"

"Ms. Prem is no longer with the company."

"Because she isn't a psycho drone willing to pull sixty hour weeks with no raise or bonus in two years?"

"Forty would have been a nice start. And when the company makes money again we'll all get raises and bonuses."

"Like we did last year?"

"C'mon, you know she wasn't getting her work done, because you've been picking up the slack for her."

"She was on *my* team. You should have discussed this with me."

"You've been a little otherwise engaged, now haven't you?"

"But it was still my job. God, you can't just use people and discard them like that."

"Actually I can. In fact I have to; the budget for my department has just been cut by a third."

"You just wrote me up, should I be worried?" said Kat, crossing her arms.

"Actually, you've been recommended for senior project manager," said Rebecca.

"What?" Kat sputtered. "You did that?"

Rebecca leaned forward and linked her hands together on her desk. "I think we both know where that came from, and why."

"What are you talking about?" said Kat, temper rising.

"Kat? Go back to your desk and calm down, before you say something you'll regret."

§

Kat did not go to her desk. She went straight to Jason's office, rapped firmly on his door and entered without waiting for an invitation. Fortunately Meredith had a dental appointment that morning, because Kat would have gone postal on her if she'd said so much as a word about "Jason," who was on the phone as she barged in, shutting the door firmly behind herself. He smiled at her hopefully as he held up the "just a minute" single digit.

"Nope," said Kat firmly, "no finger, no minute, hang it up—we gotta' talk."

"I have to go, something just came up here," Jason said into the phone. He hung up and looked up at her. "What can I do for you?"

"Did you recommend me for project manager?"

"Yes, and it's a hundred-percent merit-based promotion."

"Yeah, right. Jason, believe me, the last thing you have to worry about is me telling anybody about what happened in Seattle. In fact I'm considering hypnosis to forget it."

"Look, I'll admit I have…special needs."

"Special needs?" she said, incredulous. "My God! This is the first time the thought that there's someone for everyone actually frightens me."

"OK, so I'm a little weird. But business is business; we need to put this behind us."

At which she burst out laughing.

"What?" said Jason.

"That's too perfect," she said, wiping the tears from her eyes as she opened his door.

"What are you going to do?" he asked, more than a little worried.

Kat stopped and looked at him, realizing he probably thought her hysterical. "I don't know. But I promise it won't involve you."

§

Kat had barely collapsed into her chair when Juanita appeared in her doorway. "You heard?" she said.

Kat put her finger to her lips and indicated the wall separating her cubicle from the one formerly known as Tina's.

"Stuckie called her into her office first thing," Juanita said quietly. "Gus had to watch her clean out her desk, then escort her out of the building like a criminal."

"That's a real morale builder, isn't it?" said Kat as her phone rang. She mouthed "Rebecca" to Juanita who quickly headed back to her desk. Rebecca requested an update on a project Kat hadn't even started. She told her the truth, and said she'd get to it. As Excel opened she settled back in her chair and looked up at the air vent, trying to decide if its whistling sound was getting louder. Her phone rang and she opened it without even checking the caller ID.

Tina said, "You lookin' for me?" She didn't sound even remotely upset.

"Are you OK?" said Kat.

"I'm great. You got a new neighbor yet?"

"Yeah, a temp," said Kat, lowering her voice. "So it's obviously difficult to, you know…"

"I know," said Tina. "Call me tonight when you get home."

"Actually, I could use this really big favor, and we could talk then. Could you drive me to the Valley?"

§

At precisely four minutes past five PM, Kat was in Tina's little yellow VW as it pulled away from the curb in front of the building and entered Los Angeles rush hour traffic.

"You miss too much work," said Tina checking her mirror to change lanes, "the work you do is substandard, you distract your co-workers, inappropriate attire, bad attitude, blah, blah, blah." She ignored the blasted horn from a car she hadn't seen. "Bad attitude? Where does the bitch get that?"

"I can't imagine," said Kat.

"So I guess she could tell."

"Uh, yeah. But I don't know how someone keeps a good attitude around her."

"Gus was sweet. He was, like, 'I'm sorry, Tina,'" she said, driving intensely. "And they already have a temp in my squirrel cage?"

"Yeah, probably a fresh MBA."

"For half what they paid me, and no benefits."

"What are you going to do?" said Kat.

"Remember when you said you thought the air vents in that place were poisoning us? You were right. I was dying a little bit every day I went there."

An SUV cut them off and Tina screamed, "Fucking asshole!" and flipped him off.

"You know, that guy's probably armed," said Kat.

"Good point," Tina said, stopping for the light she missed because of the SUV. "Anyway, I've been thinking a lot, having a, you know, kind of mid-life crisis?"

"Teen, you're twenty-six."

"Twenty-five."

"And it makes your crisis *more* mid-life because you're a year younger?"

"Whatever. Do you ever wonder what it would be like to really love your job and your life?"

"Like, every day."

"Well, I'm gonna' figure out how to do it. Stuckie did me a favor."

"In other words, you have no plan."

"I have a plan," said Tina, mildly insulted. The light turned green and she accelerated away, quickly catching up to the SUV, whose driver gave her the The Look. "You know, you're right, he could have a gun," said Tina, looking very straight ahead.

"The plan?" said Kat, knowing it was next to impossible for her friend to stay on one subject for more than fifteen seconds.

"Two words: edible landscaping."

"OK," said Kat carefully.

"I go to people's houses, not farms or even places with very big yards, and plant things that look cool and that they can eat too. And not just lettuce and artichokes, bok choi, kale and chard, or tomatoes, you know, the stuff everybody thinks of. There's purslane. And orach and strawberry spinach are pretty. Fruit trees, of course, but there's like twenty berry vines that you can use for privacy, and about fifty kinds of grapes."

"Edible landscaping," said Kat, impressed.

"Fuck yes," said Tina, as she set them in the queue for the freeway onramp. "So, what's the deal with your mom? You haven't dragged me out there in a long time."

"Actually tonight I'll be meeting her solo."

"No kidding," said Tina. "When's the last time you did that?"

"I think when I first got out of school."

"You sure? I'm cool; I mean I don't have plans or anything."

"I'm sure. There's some stuff we need to talk about, some things that are long overdue. Like, twenty years overdue."

§

They sat quietly in the VW in front of Jean's house for a long minute. Kat indicated the fifteen-year-old Honda in the driveway. "She's home."

"What if she doesn't let you in?"

"If I stand right in front of the door she won't be able to see who I am and she'll open it and I'll, you

238

know, stick my foot in like a salesman so she'll have to let me in."

"I'm not the only one with a plan," said Tina.

"Exactly."

"I'll just sit here till you're inside anyway. Just in case."

"Thanks, Teen."

"BFF," said Tina, making a fist. Kat punched it.

"Everybody thinks you're this hot, stylish little babe, but you're actually a dork."

"We'll just keep that between us, OK?" said Tina.

"Deal," said Kat, smiling at her friend. "BFF."

Kat got out of the car and crossed the scruffy lawn to the little turquoise tract house's white front door. Standing away from the side view window, she rang the doorbell. A short time later the curtains parted, then she heard the door being unlocked and she waved to Tina, who waved back as she pulled away from the curb.

"Oh," said Jean when she saw her daughter on her doorstep.

"Oh? That's it?"

"Well, come in, I suppose," said Jean.

"So were we just supposed to never talk again?" said Kat as Jean, wearing a rose pastel pantsuit and slightly shabby white slippers, closed the door behind her.

They stood facing each other for a moment as the older woman struggled to find an answer.

"Well?" insisted Kat. "What is your problem?"

"I don't know what you're talking about," said Jean.

"Uh, not returning my calls?"

"Are you hungry?" Jean said, and shuffled to the kitchen.

"God, that is your answer to everything," Kat said, following after her.

"Well, it is suppertime. I cooked a chicken. Go ahead and sit down, I'll set up a place for you."

"I haven't eaten meat since I was fourteen."

"That's right. Well, I have some leftovers." Jean opened the refrigerator. "You drink beer, don't you? I don't think I have any. There's some milk, but I'm not sure how old it is." She examined the date on the milk carton. "Oh, dear, that won't do."

"Mom, I really just need to talk to you. Could you please sit down?"

Cornered, Jean reluctantly pulled a chair out across the table from her daughter.

"It's about the house, isn't it?" said Kat. "You're upset because of Aunt Ruth's house."

"You're a grown woman. What you do is your business."

"Really? Like what Aunt Ruth did was her business?"

"*That* is none of your business," snapped Jean.

"It is now. Because it's my house, and there's something seriously wrong there."

"I still don't see what that has to do with me."

"I think I got your ghost," said Kat.

"Oh, for goodness sake, what is wrong with you?"

"Good question," said Kat. "I've been thinking about that a lot lately, and I'm beginning to think a lot of it is related to the day I sat on my bicycle behind a tree across from Aunt Ruth's house and saw Ruth and Dad."

Jean was stunned.

"Say something, Mom. Talk to me, for God's sake."

"I don't know what to say."

"Anything. Try me," said Kat.

"So you've known all along?"

"I guess on some level, but not the conscious one. I learned from the best; when there's something we can't think about, it just goes away, doesn't it?"

A tear formed in the corner of Jean's eye and trickled down her cheek, followed by another. She said, "I wish that were true."

"It works sometimes. But sometimes it doesn't," said Kat. "I was afraid I'd lose them both. Then I did anyway."

"And you probably blame me," said Jean.

"When I was little and Dad didn't come home, I couldn't think of any other reason. But little by little I'm beginning to understand. We all believe in the same fairy tale, don't we? But real life has infinite versions."

"I had a right to fight for my marriage," said Jean.

"Yes, you did, but it's time to stop fighting."

"What can I do now? They're both gone."

"Maybe not. Come back to the house with me."

"To talk to a ghost."

"Yes."

"Seriously, Kat, you're worrying me. Do you know how crazy that sounds?'

"Do this for me. Please. I've never asked you to talk to me about why my father completely disappeared from our lives, and frankly, that's crazy."

"What about supper?" Jean said looking slightly bewildered, and for the first time in her life Kat realized that her mother was old.

"Put the chicken in the fridge for tomorrow. I'll fix us some pasta and open a bottle of wine."

"Do I need to change?" Jean said hopelessly.

§

They drove in silence, Kat aware of the much faster drivers zipping by on both sides of them on the freeway. She looked at her mother and thought, *This stranger.*

Finally feeling it awkward, Jean ventured, "Did you have a nice birthday?"

"Maybe the worst ever," said Kat. "Marty tried to give me food poisoning and asked if he can date Tina."

"I don't understand," said Jean, "I thought you were going out with your girlfriends on your birthday."

"That's the part you don't understand?"

"Well, you said…"

"I know what I said. Marty broke up with me."

"I'm sorry," said Jean.

"Really?"said Kat.

"I don't know, I want you to be happy."

"And you think I was happy with Marty?"

"I don't know. I don't know what makes people happy these days," said Jean actually slowing down more.

"Let's just say making me happy wasn't something Marty spent a lot of time worrying about," said Kat, looking at the needle on the speedometer hovering barely above fifty and wondering if they were going to be rear-ended by a speeding semi and roasted alive in the flaming crash.

§

Jean parked in the driveway and turned off the key, and the two looked at the house until Kat said, "All right, let's go," and opened her door.

"I can't do it," said Jean, barely able to get the words out.

"Yes you can, and you will, because we're going to do this together."

"Kat," Jean pleaded.

Kat reached over and took the keys. "I mean it Mother, we're going in. If I have to drag you from the car, you're coming in there with me."

"To talk to a ghost?" Jean repeated, knowing that saying it again wasn't going to make her daughter give her a different answer.

"To talk to me then," said Kat. She climbed out of the car and waited. Jean looked at her, sighed, and got out of the car.

"Shouldn't you lock it?" said Jean, looking bewildered.

Kat re-opened her door and pushed the button, then walked around the car and locked the driver's side. She looked at her mother, aware again of her frailty. "Come on," she said, gently taking her arm, and led her across the lawn to the dark front door.

Inside, Kat switched on the light and went to the kitchen to start the pasta water as Jean lingered in the hallway by the front door, sullen. When she woke up that morning she hadn't planned on reliving one of the most painful moments of her life, when she'd demanded that her sister leave her family alone, already knowing that "family" was gone. She heard Kat pull the cork from a wine bottle in the kitchen and said, "None for me, it will give me a headache."

Kat came out of the kitchen with two glasses filled to their brims and gave Jean one. "You don't get headaches, mother, you're a carrier."

244

"That's a mean thing to say. Why does everything have to be a joke?"

"Defense mechanism?" Kat guessed, walking back to the kitchen to make the salads. Then she realized her mother was still in the hall. "Are you planning on standing there all night?"

"I'm not comfortable here," said Jean.

"Well, you better get used to it, I'm planning on living in this house a long time. Come on, talk to me while I make our supper."

A moment later Jean made it as far as the kitchen door. She took a sip of wine.

"That's better," said Kat.

"The house looks nice," Jean grudgingly admitted. "Just the way I remembered it. I was always jealous she had such nice things."

"OK, if we're confessing stuff, I didn't understand why we didn't have the stuff she had, the clothes and car and food."

"You probably wished she was your mother."

"No," said Kat, "but I remember wishing we could live with her."

"Your father would have liked that."

"That's gross," said Kat as she dumped the pasta in the boiling water. She took a sip of wine then put her glass on the counter next to the stove and turned back to preparing their salads. "Have you ever wondered why we do the things we do, why we make the choices we make?"

"What do you mean?" Jean said as she crossed the room and sat at the table in the breakfast nook. "Life just happens, doesn't it?"

"I wonder," said Kat. "How old were you when Grandpa died? Five? Six?"

"Six. What does that have to do with anything?"

"You married a man who didn't stick around either," said Kat.

"My father didn't abandon us."

"In a way he did. Dying, running off, same difference for a six year old. Then look at me: I spent eight years with a man who may as well have been gone."

"I never thought of it like that," said Jean. "So are you saying we don't have a choice?"

"I don't know, but if we don't pay attention we're liable to keep repeating this stuff."

The women were quiet for a moment, one stirring the pasta water, the other carefully considering her wine glass. Jean broke the silence. "Well, even if that's true, it's too late for me."

"You wouldn't like to meet someone?"

"I'm too old…"

"That's silly," Kat interjected.

"…and too angry," finished her mother.

"That could be a problem," said Kat, and they both laughed, Kat realizing how good it felt for them to be on the same side.

§

Later, their plates licked clean and the bottle nearly gone, they sat in the living room in the light of a pair of candles Kat had lit on the coffee table.

"I would be huge if I ate like this every night," said Jean.

"Right, you'd be a total hippo. God, Mother, you haven't weighed more than a hundred and five in your life."

"Well, it was delicious. You've turned into quite the little cook."

"That's me, quite the little cook," said Kat as she tried to give her mother more wine.

"Oh, dear, no," Jean said, covering her glass. "If I drink any more I won't care where I go to the bathroom." Then she giggled.

"Mother! I'm shocked," said Kat, as she poured the rest into her own glass.

"I'm not a total prig," said Jean. "I know you think I am."

"I don't know what you are, or rather who," said Kat. "I mean, I know you worked and we always had enough to eat and clothes on our backs, but you were this cipher. And you always had this—I'm not sure how to say it exactly—shadow of sadness."

"Until someone has really and truly broken your heart, you'll never understand."

"I'm learning," said Kat. "Until recently I didn't think I could ever feel that way about someone, like there was a black hole in my heart. I guess that's why I settled for Marty."

"I couldn't stand him," said Jean, then covered her mouth. "Oh, dear, I shouldn't be drinking this much wine."

"It's OK. I finally realized I couldn't stand him either, let alone love him, at least in that way I've always dreamed of. But I know why I stayed with him so long; I thought he'd never leave me. And then he did anyway. Mom, I need for you to tell me the truth. Did Dad really never want to see us again?"

"Your father and I agreed it would be better if he stayed out of our lives for good."

"The two of you decided, or you decided?"

"I'm sorry, Kat. You were so little. I can see that now. But my heart wasn't just broken, it was shattered; there were no pieces left to pick up."

"And for twenty years you've lived with the bitterness."

"This is something you can never understand, because you weren't a twin. She was literally a part of me from the first moment our hearts beat." She stopped and listened to the house. "And you think she's here now, talking to you?"

"She hasn't said anything."

"But you think you've seen her."

"I know I have."

"Assuming there is something here, why would anything I say matter?"

"Maybe it won't. And you're right, perhaps this is all just more of my confusing reality and all the pretty stories. And whether or not something or someone is here, anything we can do or say may not help. But if it only helps us, it'll be worthwhile."

"All right," Jean said, yawning. "I'm exhausted; I feel like I've been through something."

"We have," said Kat.

"I don't even have a toothbrush."

"I have a new one, still in the wrapper."

§

That night Kat snuggled in, her back to her nice warm mother, in a way she hadn't for twenty-five years, a way she only now remembered. Surprised, Jean stroked her daughter's hair, then lay back and listened to the quiet night sounds of the house, its wooden joints murmuring as they contracted. It was easy to imagine this house as a living thing. She looked around the dark empty room, not sure what she was supposed to be looking for. Twice again she tried to sleep, but each time felt the weight of words unsaid. Finally she rose up on one elbow, listening with every bit of will in her body, until she understood this was about faith.

"Ruth, if you're there," Jean said hesitantly, "I'm sorry. I just felt so hurt and betrayed, and afraid that I'd lose Kat too." She held her breath, half expecting a response. "I tried so hard to understand why you, of all people, would want to hurt me, until I realized the reason there was no answer to that is that you couldn't have. I don't know if he ever really loved me in that way, where the earth moves, but I'm sure it was like that for you, and…" Jean's voice cracked and the tears came. "It was just so hard for me accept that. It's still…" Jean stumbled, fighting tears. "So hard." Was that a stirring in the room, or just the wind moving a curtain? She continued, struggling with the words. "But you always were and always will be a part of me. I'm sorry I couldn't find a way to tell you then that I still loved you. I mean, I know it's a little late," she said, laughing through her tears, almost expecting to hear her sister immediately sharing her laughter the way they finished each other's sentences, as if they yet shared one heart.

"Anyway, I'm sorry I couldn't tell you then that I still love you."

Again Jean listened in the silence of the night, until she lay down beside her daughter, not realizing that the younger woman's eyes were open, and fell into the deep peaceful sleep of an innocent heart.

fifteen

Kat entered the kitchen in a blouse, skirt and heels as her mother wrapped the unfinished half of the cookie in a napkin and put it in her purse.

"There's plenty, you can take some that aren't half eaten too," said Kat.

"Oh dear, I don't know. Well, all right, just a few," said Jean, taking the napkin from her purse and adding two more from the plate. "They are delicious. You have a gift. I don't know where you get it, certainly not from me."

Kat said, "It's not like I'm curing cancer or anything."

"Some of the most important moments in my life happened over a lovely meal, with my family when I was a girl, or in a restaurant with your father." She takes another cookie from the plate (purely to use as an example, of course). "The taste of a lemon cookie," she said dipping it in her coffee, "or a perfect cup of coffee." she took a bite, closing her eyes, "…sends me back and I relive the moment all over again. It's a gift, Kat. Don't ever forget that."

Kat poured herself a cup of coffee and sat down next to her mother. "So, are you OK?" she said, taking a cookie.

"That's a wonderful bed; I haven't slept likc that in years."

"I'm glad, but you know that isn't what I meant. Did you see anything last night?"

"No. Maybe it's not my ghost after all. She was your Godmother."

"I didn't know that," said Kat, stunned. "Why didn't you tell me?"

"I thought I did. Perhaps you were too young to remember."

"And then…"

"And then I didn't feel like talking about it."

"Mom, last night? I was awake. I heard you talking to her."

Jean looked, down, embarrassed. "But it's true I didn't see her. I don't know who I was talking too, maybe to myself. I did feel something though, a kind of peace. What do they call it, closure? You were right. It's time." Kat put her hand on her mother's, and the old woman looked at it, surprised and tears rolled down her cheeks. "I know I may not have been so great as a mother."

"You were an OK mom. Of course, you were the only one I had, so I can't really compare, but I didn't end up so bad. I have a nice life, and I have you to thank for it, right? What I could really use now is a friend."

"We learn a little more every day how to be us, don't we?" Jean said, putting her hand on her daughter's. "Even if some of us are slow learners." She looked at the clock. "Goodness, look at the time. Are you late for work?"

"Not if you drop me," said Kat.

§

The day actually went well. Rebecca called Kat into her office first thing for a very friendly and businesslike meeting to talk about wrapping up her projects before her promotion and move to the new department. And the lemon drop cookies were a huge hit with Gus and everyone in the lunchroom; people were still talking about them when she left at the end of the day. But it was jarring and weird knowing a temp was sitting at Tina's desk. Then she looked up at the air vent and was as sure as she had ever been in her life about what she had to do.

All this was on her mind when she stepped down to the curb from the bus and started walking past the Starbucks parking lot. Then she stopped. *Something feels different*, she thought, looking across the lot at the little bakery. But nothing was. They were open, but empty as usual, except for the girl, who appeared to be reading a paperback at the table by the window.

Kat booted her laptop as soon as she got home and worked for three hours on a very special spreadsheet, with frequent forays onto the Web for survey data and statistics, and a couple of snack missions to the kitchen in place of dinner. When she was done she printed it out, read it for errors, and printed it again.

Then she started baking. First came the cookies, her richest peanut butter, a batch of chocolate chip with flakes of cinnamon-y Mexican chocolate, and the lemon drops that had been such a hit that day (and which she'd actually only just invented). Coconut followed the others onto the cooling racks, then biscotti, and finally ginger snaps so snappy they exploded in your mouth. She hadn't planned on making them, but at four AM she finished icing a tray of petites fours, then put her head down on the kitchen table "just for a moment," and was instantly fast asleep. So deeply did she sleep, she didn't feel the gentle ghostly hand stroke her hair. Angel or godmother? Maybe both.

Kat woke at seven-thirty, surrounded by cookies and beautiful little cakes. She stumbled outside to pick up the paper and, remembering it was trash pick-up day, wheeled the bins to the curb,. Then she took her longest shower in years, after which she washed down eggs and a muffin with a quadruple shot of espresso mixed with steamed milk, vanilla and a fat cube of dark crystallized raw sugar. Thus fortified, she dressed for work, carefully packed a pastry box with two each of her previous night's creations, called in sick, and stepped out into the glorious Los Angeles morning with the pastry box in one hand and a thick manila envelope in the other, a woman on a mission.

Walking to the corner, Kat was struck by three things: the beauty of the Jacarandas framed by the intense blue of the sky, the faint scent of ocean one got in LA on especially clear days, tinged by the floral scents wafting from her neighbors' yards, and the fact that she was Kat Young. Not Beryl Markham flying her tiny silver plane over Kenya. Not a lovely Mexican girl sneaking out to meet her lover. Not a ravishing beauty tied to a yardarm by pirates. Just Kat, on her way to the most important meeting of her life.

§

Laila, because that was her name, looked up from her magazine when the doorbell dinged and Kat walked into the otherwise empty shop.

"Hi," said Kat.

"Hi," said Laila cautiously. "You want to try the coffee again?"

"I don't think so," said Kat.

"Then…?"

Kat put the pastry box on the table, and stuck out her hand. "I'm Kat Young."

The girl looked at her hand like it was a foreign object, then said, "I'm Laila," as she accepted the handshake.

"I'd like to speak to the owner," said Kat.

"You remember I gave you your money back?" Laila said, alarmed.

"It's OK, I remember," said Kat.

"Can I just get you something else? We got new milk yesterday, and it hasn't been out of the fridge once."

Somehow Kat wasn't surprised to hear this. "No thanks, I just want to speak to the owner."

"My father's not that easy to talk to?" Laila was now clearly agitated. "And I'm really sorry about what happened."

"Laila? I promise it's not about what happened. Could I please just speak to him?"

Defeated, the girl picked up her phone and speed dialed, speaking in Farsi when it was answered. Kat gathered she filled him in fairly accurately, because a moment later she could hear him shouting at her. She lowered the phone. "Did you have to go to the hospital?"

"No, I didn't," said Kat.

Laila relayed this information, then turned to Kat again. "He says he can be here in ten minutes. Can you wait?"

"No problem."

Message conveyed, Laila closed her phone. She squinted at Kat uncomfortably. "You sure you don't want anything?"

Kat looked at the Twinkies, Snowballs and Ding Dongs in the display case, fairly certain they'd been there since her visit with Marty, and said, "I'm good." She went to the window and looked at the Starbucks across the lot. There was an empty parking space directly in front of the door.

Precisely ten minutes later, Manny Shiraz, a short, exceedingly dignified man in an elegant Italian suit and tie, exploded into the shop, already talking. "I am Manny Shirazi. I am so sorry, madam. I have told this girl many times that perishable items must always be refrigerated. Thanks God you have not been seriously sickened. I assure you that any expenses you have incurred will be compensated."

"Thank you, Mr. Shirazi, but, as I promised Laila, that's not why I'm here."

"You're not going to sue me?"

"No," Kat said firmly, "I just wanted to introduce myself." She held out her hand, saying, "I'm Kat Young." Then, when they'd shaken hands, she picked up the pastry box and said, "and I'd like for you to try

257

one of these." She opened it and offered it to him, alarming him further.

"Were these purchased here?"

"No, I made them. Please, just take one."

He took one, humoring her, and nibbled at it, raising an eyebrow. "Good," he said, then took a real bite.

Kat offered the box to Laila. "Would you like to try one?"

"No thanks."

"Take one," Manny said sternly.

Laila quickly took a cookie and tried a small bite. "Good," she said uncomfortably.

Kat put the open box on the table and picked up the envelope and took out the spreadsheet, alarming Manny anew.

"What is this?"

"It's a business plan. Just look it over?"

He took it and scanned it, absently taking another cookie from the box. "A business plan for this shop? We have a plan."

"Uh huh. I live nearby, I can see how well that's working."

Manny read on. "This would be nice, if it could be true. Where did you get this?"

"I prepared it. I usually do them for multi-million-dollar projects, but the principles are the same: location, product, presentation, service."

"Location?" sniffed Manny. "This is terrible location, next to bloody Starbucks."

"Actually, that could be a plus. Starbucks doesn't offer any fresh baked goods. This could be an excellent location if we focused on onsite freshly baked cookies and pastries."

"We?"

"Yes, I'm proposing a partnership."

Manny took another cookie, a coconut, and turned it over in his hand before taking a bite. "These are remarkable. However you're proposing a partnership with no investment on your part."

Kat was glad she'd worn her suit. "Mr. Shirazi, I know how to use those fancy ovens, And I know how this business should be run. Every day I pass your shop and there's never anyone in here but your daughter. The place could have tremendous potential with a fresh direction. As it is, you have 100% of what may as well be an empty storefront."

Manny opened the business plan again, speaking as he scanned it. "My wife, Laila's mother, is with God. I bought this place to teach the girl some responsibility."

Laila sneered. "You won it in a poker game!"

"That's not precisely true," he said, trying to hold onto his dignity. "But it was in payment of a debt, accepted with Laila in mind."

"I would love for her to be here to help. I think she's very bright," said Kat diplomatically.

"You do?" Manny said, the surprise in his voice obvious enough to cause Laila to roll her eyes. He looked at her and she opened her hands in a "What are you waiting for?" gesture. He chose another cookie from the pastry box, a lemon, and took a bite.

"You really made these?"

"In my kitchen last night."

Every success Manny had in life, and he'd had many, had been the result of recognizing an opportunity and acting on it without hesitating. He saw one here, and made a decision. "I'll make coffee and we'll talk." He went behind the counter and started to fill the coffee machine.

§

When Kat got back to her house her feet were barely touching the ground. Manny had kept the remaining cookies in their pastry box (her idea), but more importantly, her spreadsheet (his idea), so he could go over it with his attorney and draft a contract for their partnership. It very much appeared Kat had her bakery. There was also a shoe box leaning on her front door.

She picked it up gingerly. There was no reason someone would leave a bomb on her porch, but caution still seemed to be called for when handling an unsolicited package left at your door. It had to have been hand-delivered—the only thing written on the lid was her name. Shaking it revealed nothing, whatever was inside was well-packed. The Scotch tape peeled off easily and she carefully lifted the lid. The box was packed with tissue, and she immediately knew what was in it.

In the days following the Cooper debacle she'd had an unusually hard time putting it out of her mind, but the craziness at work with Tina, Stevens and Rebecca and dealing with her mother and their "ghost," had helped tremendously. Finally, her epiphany about the bakery, and the subsequent flurry of work to prepare had pushed it completely into that shadowy area she was so expert at ignoring. Now here it was back, and she found it terrifically annoying. Without bothering to look, she marched it to the curb. *As if just dropping off this fucking corny glass shoe is going to make me fall back into his (and his fucking wife's) bed with my legs spread.* She lifted the lid on the blue bin and tossed it in, thinking, *Recycle it into something useful, like a pickle jar.*

§

Her first call was to Tina. "Remember when you were talking about imagining what it would feel like to really love your job and your life? Well, I imagined it, and it looks like I made it happen." The decision was to

261

celebrate over Thai food (and Thai beers), and Tina was actually early picking her up.

As they studied their menus, Kat said, "You're so on time now, should I be worried about you?"

"I'll get over it soon as I start real work," said Tina. "I'm kind of losing it—I went for two runs today."

"I thought you *were* working. The edible landscaping deal?"

"I mean when I start actually landscaping. I've been setting up the Web site and working on linking it to other sites. I realized today what I was doing was sort of the same as my old job, but with a bigger cubicle."

"Your apartment isn't that small."

"Compared to your house. OK, I have a little house envy. But there's nothing I can do about it now. For one thing, it doesn't look like any of my aunts are dying, and they're all, like, breeders, so there are dozens of cousins ahead of me when they do kick, so I'm basically screwed."

"There is so much wrong with what you just said I wouldn't even know where to begin."

The waitress appeared with Thai beers and two frosty glasses on a tray. She put the beer and glasses on the table, then took out her pad and pen. "Ready to order?"

Tina turned back to the menu. "I think we're starting with *Tom Yum Kung* soup." She looked at Kat. "Right?"

"Excellent," said Kat.

"Mild, medium or hot?" asked the waitress.

"Thai hot," said Tina.

"That hot," said the waitress, noting this on her pad.

"Uh, I hope so," said Tina absently, reading the menu. "And *Som Tam*," she said, using the Thai for papaya salad.

"Mild, medium…" began the waitress.

"*Phet Thai*," interrupted Tina, using the Thai word for beyond spicy.

"OK," said the waitress, her tone registering disapproval as she wrote "*phet Thai*" again on her pad.

"And *Pad Kee Mao*," said Tina, finishing with the insanely hot drunken noodles as she closed her menu.

This was too much for the waitress, who switched to Thai herself, "White people don't like this. Too much spice. Everything you've ordered has too much spice for a white person."

Tina fixed her with a baleful stare, responding in kind, both in tone and in Thai. "I don't see a white person at this table, it's just me and my best friend. Is there a problem?"

"No, no problem," the waitress said in Thai, her raised eyebrow and sing-song tone indicating "We'll see about that," as she wrote "*Phet Thai*" next to *Pad Kee Mao* on her pad.

"What was that about?" Kat said as the waitress returned to the kitchen.

"She's an asshole," said Tina filling her glass, "talking about white people. I told her I didn't see any, just me and my best friend."

"Thank you," said Kat, genuinely touched.

"Not insane people need to stick together," said Tina. She took a long swallow of beer, then wiped her lips in a satisfied manner. "So tell me everything that happened."

"I already told you."

"Tell me again. It's nice to see you like this."

"Like how?" said Kat.

"Excited about living," said Tina. "Hanging with you has been kind of mood challenging lately."

"I'm sorry."

"No need," said Tina, "TWFAF."

"But you're right, I am. Excited about living. Weird. What if everything we've been taught, as women I mean, is wrong?"

"I'm self-taught. No way was I going to be like my mother," said Tina. "So, spill, what happened?"

"I did it. I really did it. I wrote a proposal for that little shop around the corner, presented it to the owner, after finally convincing his daughter who is scared shitless of him that I wasn't there to sue them for food poisoning, and he bought it! He has his lawyer drawing up an agreement."

"The guy's from Iran?"

"Uh, yeah," allowed Kat.

"They can be slippery," warned Tina.

"Well, at least he's not Chinese, right?"

"Yeah," agreed Tina, "They're really bad." Then she saw Kat giving her a look. "What?"

"Remember the argument you had with that waitress two minutes ago?"

"You're right," said Tina, suitably chastised, "I have known some pretty nice Persians."

"He seems really nice and very professional and down to earth. Most importantly, he needs me more than I need him. Or at least as much. I've passed that place a hundred times and I've never seen a customer in there. Anyway, I didn't just fall off the turnip truck; I know how to read a contract."

"When are you going to quit your job?"

"We're supposed to meet again on Thursday to go over everything and sign. Assuming everything looks right, Friday."

"God I wish I could see Stuckie's face when you tell her."

"Actually, I'm out of her clutches anyway," said Kat, instantly regretting her words.

"Why?" said Tina, suddenly alert.

"I kind of got promoted."

"What do you mean 'kind of'?" said Tina.

"OK, I got a promotion. This was supposed to be my last week."

"Great," said Tina, "I get fired and you get promoted. When were you going to tell me?"

"I don't know," said Kat, embarrassed. "When you were back on your feet?"

"I'm fine," said Tina. "And you're a good friend." She raised her beer glass. "To best friends."

"To best friends," said Kat raising hers to touch Tina's as the waitress appeared with a steaming bowl of soup on a flaming stand. She ladled each of them a healthy serving, then stood back with a smirk on her face. Recognizing the challenge, Kat and Tina picked up their spoons and tasted it. The soup was beyond spicy, a bowl of liquid fire. "Oh, my God," they said in unison, tears forming in their eyes.

"More beers?" said the waitress sweetly.

§

About ten, Kat climbed out of Tina's car and walked unsteadily across her lawn, the result of the two additional beers each of them had enjoyed, way more than she'd ever drunk on a school night. Tina waited till Kat was on her porch and had her key in the door before she waved and drove off. Kat opened the door, then looked back at the trash bins at the curb. Was Tuesday the pickup day or tomorrow? *Whatever,* she decided, she'd drag them back up the driveway in the morning, and it certainly wasn't because she wanted to see if the glass slipper was still there. She hoped it wasn't. No, really.

Not surprisingly, Kat fell asleep as soon as her head hit the pillow. What was surprising was that the music box began playing *Somewhere My Love* precisely at three AM. Kat had grown used to sleeping in the house, to the sounds the house made as its various wooden parts expanded and contracted and flexed with the wind. She also assumed the house poltergeist would find peace now that the twins, one living, one departed, had hopefully reconciled. But, as her mother had said, maybe it wasn't her ghost. Kat opened her eyes and shuddered, the first twinges of the next morning's hangover creeping into her head. "Aunt Ruth," she began as she propped herself up on one elbow, but stopped when she saw her spectral godmother at the foot of her bed, a cupcake with a small glowing candle cupped in her hands.

Kat remembered her birthday wish, and tears rolled from her eyes. "I really liked him," she said, and Ruth smiled gently. Did she nod as well before she vanished? Kat was only sure that she was gone. She lay back and covered her eyes with her arm. Was this how it would always be? Prince rides in. Prince sweeps you off your feet. Prince kicks you to the curb. Or was it a symptom, something in her?

She swung her bare legs over the side of the bed and sat up, wiping the tears from her face with her arm, wondering again if today was pickup day for the recycle bin. She made it as far as the door when she remembered she was barefoot, to say nothing of

267

wearing only a tank top and boy-short panties. She got a pair of crew socks from the hamper and pulled on her robe.

Kat slipped out the front door after catching a glimpse of herself in the hall mirror. *That's a great look.* The night was so still it was hard to believe she lived in one of the biggest cities on earth. The sprinkler had just finished so the lawn and walk glistened, and the soles of her socks were quickly wet. The lid on the blue bin was indeed closed, but the black one was open, meaning the pickup had been that day; the blue bin had just slammed shut when the truck flipped it back to the curb. Still, she stepped into the street and lifted the lid. *Empty.*

She sighed, *feeling* empty and cold, especially her feet. *He wins again*, she thought. *I'm standing in the effing street at three AM, in my socks.* She looked down at her feet. *Wet socks.* Then she caught of glint of light from the gutter behind the recycle bin, a glint of glass. Pushing the bin aside, she picked it up—it was the heel of the glass slipper, broken off the way a heel breaks when you catch the heel of a real shoe in a transom. *Which it isn't. Real, that is*, Kat reminded herself. She pulled the bin out further and saw the rest of it, broken in half at the instep. She picked the pieces up and looked at them in her hand, remembering how thrilled she'd been at this grand romantic gesture.

Inside, she stripped off her soggy socks and dried her feet on her robe, then padded into her bedroom, where she placed the shards of glass next to the music box. *A perfect metaphor*, she thought.

sixteen

The week passed in a whirl. Realizing she was now immune to Rebecca, Kat rather enjoyed her last few days. Of course, her boss assumed her cheerful attitude was because of her promotion and was suitably hurt by it. Rebecca had not only never gotten that she wasn't a people person, she saw herself as something of a bright fairy, buzzing from flower to flower bringing happiness and order to everything she touched. Well, on good days. Bad days, she felt she was a fat, slovenly ogre with no real friends that no man would ever want to touch. If Kat had known this she might have made more of an effort, but she'd long since given up trying to understand her beyond what she needed to do to get by with the woman. And now it didn't matter, she felt positively liberated.

True to his word, Manny had their contract ready on Thursday, and Kat was pleased to see she'd been right about him when she'd had dinner with Tina; she felt it was very fair. She'd draw a modest salary against future profit for the first year, and if by the end of the year they realized the very reasonable numbers they'd agreed on, she'd not only own half the bakery, but they would begin looking for additional locations. He also agreed to do a makeover on the shop. Nothing major, she was very happy with the kitchen, just fresh paint and tables and chairs, including two more sets for outside on nice days, which Los Angles has an embarrassment of. Oh, and a new sign, reflecting the new name, *Happy Endings*.

Kat gave Rebecca her two-weeks notice on Friday, with no further explanation beyond "it's time for a change." As she expected, per company policy, Gus saw her out immediately. He told her he'd miss her. "You're just going to miss the cookies," she said. "No, I'll miss you," said Gus. "And the cookies." She gave him a hug. Juanita got one too, even though she'd see her Saturday when she was planning on checking out the shop. Todd got a handshake. *Why not?*

§

Caspian Corner officially closed on Saturday, when the renovation began, with the planned grand reopening the following Saturday. This gave Kat a week to plan her menu, supervise the renovation and design the new sign, choose the new furniture, plates, bags, napkins and plastic ware, and design and print five hundred door hangers offering a free cookie and coffee on the impending Saturday. Tina offered to distribute the door hangers, a task she spread over several days in conjunction with her now compulsive jogging.

It was on one of these forays, a loop that took her as far as a neighboring Starbucks, that Tina saw the red pickup truck with the telltale crumpled fender. Cooper was just being served. She leaned against the door of his truck with her arms crossed, so she could give him a second serving.

"Hey, asshole!" she said when he came out of the shop.

When Cooper said, "Hi, Tina," he was as close to losing his cool as he'd ever been. She continued to lean on his truck, blocking his way, and he resigned himself to the inevitable. "So, I guess you heard," he said.

"You have a lot of fucking nerve," said Tina.

"Actually, it's the opposite problem."

"I didn't think anyone in the world could do it, but you managed to stomp all the hope out of the most romantic person in the world."

"I'm sorry," he said lamely.

"You're sorry? What the fuck? You're fucking sorry?"

"I don't know what to do," he said.

"You could stop thinking with your dick. Married men who lie to women so they can grab a quick fuck

272

should be castrated," Tina showed no sign of being ready to move from her station.

"That's an interesting philosophy. Fortunately I'm not married."

"The hell you aren't," she sneered.

"No, Tina, I'm really not."

"Then what was that horror film at your house?"

"Good description. That would be my literally insane ex who doesn't understand, believe or accept that we're divorced, no matter how carefully or forcefully it's explained to her by her attorney, doctor, the police and, not incidentally, myself."

"Oh, right, the crazy 'ex' excuse."

"Not excuse crazy; medically, really truly crazy. I've got the paperwork."

"Why didn't you say something?"

"I thought I had time. Sally's institutionalized, but that night she took a walk. It hadn't happened before."

"That's not exactly what I meant," said Tina.

"OK, I'm not great about talking about stuff, personal stuff, and my baggage doesn't exactly fit in the overhead compartment. It's a lot to ask of somebody."

"Kat isn't just somebody. You never gave her a chance," said Tina.

Cooper didn't know what to say, so he didn't say anything, and Tina shook her head in disgust. "Here," she said, handing him a door hanger as she stomped off. "In case you manage to grow a pair."

§

Kat and Manny watched two workmen on ladders hang the new sign, which read **Happy Endings**, as an electrician wired an exhaust fan above the door.

"We'll never be ready in time," said Manny.

"A little higher," Kat said to the guy on the right. He made the adjustment and she gave him a thumbs up.

"I don't understand this fan," said Manny, as the electrician capped off the wires.

"Everyone who walks by is going to smell cookies. Especially anyone who goes in there," Kat said, indicating the Starbucks.

"OK, this is good," admitted Manny, as Tina crossed the parking lot and joined them.

"Back for more hangers," said Tina, admiring the new sign.

Kat said, "That's great, but you've already done, like, four hundred, I can do the rest."

"I'd just be running in circles anyway," Tina said, adding, "cool sign."

"Like it?" asked Kat.

"I love it."

The two men climbed down. Impressed by Tina's tiny running shorts and tank top, they stood back behind her, to "evaluate their work." One of them gave

Kat a knowing smirk. "You know what a 'happy ending' means, right?"

"What? What does it mean?" said Manny, smelling trouble.

"I think it means living happily ever after," said Kat. "What do *you* think it means?"

"Just what you said, lady," the workman agreed, and started packing up his tools.

"Guess who I saw," Tina asked Kat conspiratorially.

"If we lived in Mayberry I could probably answer that question in less than five minutes."

"Mr. Red Truck."

Kat wasn't prepared for this. "Did you talk to him?"

"Not feeling so sarcastic now, are we?"

"Come on, Tina, what happened?"

Laila, ferrying supplies to the storeroom from her father's car, came out of the shop and greeted Tina cheerfully. Kat barely gave her friend a chance to respond as she dragged her into the shop and pushed her into a chair at the corner table. "OK, what did you say?"

"I told him he's a dick, and married guys who do what he did should be castrated."

"Wow, you said that?"

"Yep."

"I guess he deserved it."

"Maybe."

"What do you mean, 'maybe'?"

"He says he's not married."

"I saw his wife. She literally tried to tear my hair out."

"He claims it was his crazy <u>ex</u>-wife who tried to tear your hair out."

"Right, the crazy ex excuse," Kat scoffed.

"Exactly what I said."

Laila came back in lugging a box filled with bags of sugar, and Tina waited until she was in the back before saying, "He said it isn't an excuse, that he would show me the paperwork for when she was, like, committed."

"Why didn't he tell me?"

"'Cause he's a stupid guy?"

"More like a coward," said Kat.

"We discussed that too."

Laila came back out of the storeroom. "You guys want anything?"

"Thanks, we're OK," said Kat, and waited till she'd gone outside.

"Did you see him at a Starbucks?" said Kat.

"Yeah," said Tina. "I guess now he's afraid to go to the one in his own neighborhood."

"He doesn't live in this neighborhood," said Kat. "Long story."

"So, what are you going to do?" said Tina.

"I'm not going to do anything. I'm going to open my shop, get on with my life, and maybe go back to

276

reading those stupid books where everybody is after the same thing."

"OK," Tina said, stretching the syllables. The Kinko's box with the flyers was beside her chair on the floor, and she reached in and took out the last of them, about a hundred. She showed them to Kat. "So, I will take care of these."

"Thanks, Teen," said Kat.

"No problem." Tina got to her feet.

"No, I mean about…"

Laila came back in with more sugar, very interested in their conversation thanks to her newly developing chick radar.

"…that other thing," said Kat, finishing her sentence cryptically. "Thanks for, you know, sticking up for me."

"What friends are for," said Tina. "Well, I better get going," she said, indicating the flyers. "I've got a date with a lot of doorknobs."

"Uh, did you give him one of those?" asked Kat.

Tina stopped at the door. "Should I have?"

"Doesn't really matter one way or the other."

"Right," smiled Tina, reading her as easily as the menu at a Thai restaurant.

§

That night Kat had been too buzzed to sleep, tossing and turning, her head filled with doubts, fears and recipes. When she finally slept, she had the dream she thought she wouldn't be having anymore, only for the first time she was completely alone. She walked to the edge of the canyon. There weren't even any crows. A sharp wind blew her hair across her face, whipping her long full skirt around her ankles. *Long full skirt?* She looked down and saw she was wearing what appeared to be a white cotton nightgown from the late Victorian period that laced up the front with very pretty ribbons, and she was barefoot. *Weird.* She looked around. No horsemen, no fathers, no aunts. *What am I doing here?*

Then, just like that, she knew she wasn't alone. She didn't see anyone, but she knew. A gentle hand stroked her hair and, though she didn't see her, she knew Ruth was there, that there was a reason for everything and everything had a reason and she felt warm and safe, although she wished she were back in her bed because she was so tired, and the shop opening was tomorrow. Then, just as surely as she'd known Ruth was with her, she knew he was there as well, and she turned and Cooper was standing very close to her, so close she could feel the heat of his body. *You should have told me,* she thought. *I know,* he thought, and Kat was amazed that they could communicate just by thinking. Then she knew he was going to take her in his arms and she surrendered to this, waking with her arms wrapped around her pillow.

"Aunt Ruth?" she yawned, are you there?"

Silence. But she was wide awake now and sat up.

"Do you want to play cards, or something?" she said, wondering if ghosts have a sense of humor. And she wondered if the dream meant she would see him again, and she wondered what she would say to him if she did. She went to the bureau, to the music box and the broken slipper, and picked up two of the pieces and tried to fit them together. It was a remarkably clean break, only a few tiny shards were missing. She thought she had some superglue in the kitchen drawer filled with tools and the tape measure and flashlight and batteries. She took the pieces there, placing them on the counter as she rummaged for the little plastic bottle. It was in the very back of the drawer, on top of an antique brass key, obviously old, but surprisingly shiny, as if it had been routinely polished.

Back in the bedroom, the music box seemed an appropriate place for the key, and a few bars of the song played when she lifted the lid to place it there. She picked up the heel side of the glass slipper, squeezed a few drops of the clear goop on the break, and joined the two pieces, holding them as she counted to sixty. She gave it an extra ten seconds, then gently placed it next to the music box. She repeated the process with the toe part. And the welds held, although the cracks were clearly visible. *That's OK,* she thought, remembering the metaphor.

Back in bed, she was about to turn out the light, but something was nagging at her. She slipped out of bed again and opened the music box, leaving it playing as she took the key to her study and tried it on the steamer trunk. It slid easily into the lock, which opened with a satisfying click. She released the hasp and lifted the lid.

A lifetime was there, tickets for trips long since traveled and programs for shows long closed, diplomas and awards and scrapbooks with photos spanning the previous century, and a stack of letters tied with a red silk ribbon.

When Kat touched them she might have heard a sigh from deep inside the house, or it might have just been the music box winding down. She sat back with the packet in her lap and gently slipped the ribbon off. The paper was dry, but not as old as most of the other documents in the trunk. The envelopes were all addressed to Ruth, at this address, with no return address. The postmarks were mostly from Los Angeles, although there were some marked San Francisco, and a few from Chicago and New York, the most recent twenty years ago. She slipped the folded paper from the top envelope and opened it, instantly knowing whose hand the tight cursive writing had belonged to.

Ruth, my <u>so</u> dearest person,

This is just to tell you I love you— I wish there were some new way, some new words—but there just ar<u>en</u>'t, so this must suffice. I lay awake a long time last night, thinking about you, & us. And I woke early this morning with that indescribable a<u>che</u> for you—all else loses significance, and the only thing which matters is that we be together, somehow. The only wrong thing in life I can find at present is that we ev<u>er</u> have to be separated.   I love you so incredibly much. You're so much a part of me now you seem to <u>be</u> me, & without you I'm pretty lost and empty.

I love you so much, as time goes on sometimes it's almost more than I can bear—my love has grown to true worship and adoration—I find myself remembering you, in mien and action, when we're apart. And when we're together sometimes I can't take my eyes off you. You're everything I want and need and crave—you're <u>harmony</u> and joy and thrill and peace all mingled. There's never been anything like it, Ruthie—believe me. I know this is the most difficult decision you've ever had to make, and I'll wait forever, if need be—but I hope we won't have to! I love you.

Your Carl.

Overwhelmed, Kat carefully slid the letter back into its envelope, replaced the ribbon on the packet of letters, gently returned them to the trunk and locked it. In the bedroom she put the key back in the music box and closed the lid, deciding not to wind it again for the time being. Resting her hand on the bureau, she looked at the mangled glass slipper, her father's words and the enormity of the decision her aunt had faced weighing on her. So much heartbreak.

seventeen

After the revelation of her father's letter, sleep had been out of the question. Anyway she'd planned on being up at four to prepare for the opening, so she got dressed, walked up to the shop and fired up the ovens.

At seven-thirty Manny arrived with Laila, who was suitably sleepy—she'd never been there before ten, and frequently hadn't bothered to open till elevenish. Kat ran home to shower, barely making it back for their eight AM opening (hastily putting on some lipstick in the shop's restroom).

Laila had stopped Manny from making coffee, insisting she knew how to do it correctly now, and he had voiced his approval at the results, something of a first in their relationship. In fact, he was on his second cup when Kat returned, and he'd enjoyed three by eight-thirty, plus two peanut butter cookies, a lemon bar and a cupcake, putting his caffeine and sugar rush in high gear.

The door was open, the new tables were out front and the Grand Opening! banner was furled proudly across the front window as the three watched customers coming and going at Starbucks. Manny stopped pacing for a moment to choose another cookie. Laila said, "Dad, you're going to make yourself sick."

"I'm nervous," he said, but put the cookie back on the rack.

"You can't put it back there after you handled it," scolded the daughter, and Kat smiled at her prodigy's progress.

"Look," said Laila, indicating a woman who had just exited the Starbucks with a huge cardboard cup, heading straight towards them.

"She's probably just parked over here," Manny said gloomily.

She hadn't. The new electric bell sounded as she entered, and Happy Endings had its first official customer. "God, it smells amazing in here," she said, seeing Kat pull a sheet of ginger snaps from one of the ovens. "I have this," she said, showing Laila one of the door hangers.

"It's good for a free cookie and cup of coffee," said Laila.

"I already got a coffee," she said, showing her the Starbucks cup. "I really like this thing they have with pumpkin spice?"

"I know what you mean," said Kat as she put the cookie sheet on the cooling rack. "I liked them so much I tried making them with this fresh organic pumpkin extract I found? We also grind the spices fresh for each cup."

"Well, I'll have to try yours next time," said the woman, impressed. "Are those ginger cookies?"

"With fresh crystallized ginger," said Laila proudly. Manny barely recognized his daughter.

"I'll have one of those, and the chocolate chip look amazing. Let me have one of those too." She opened her purse. "How much will that be?"

"Since you're our first official customer, they're both complimentary," said Kat, and Customer #1 took her cookies and Starbucks coffee out and sat at one of the new outdoor tables as Customers #2 and #3 entered, door hangers in hand.

Manny stopped pacing.

By eleven-thirty there was a line snaking twenty feet from the door and Kat called Tina to ask her to help out. Then Manny's phone rang. Speaking angrily in Farsi, he took the call to the back of the shop, and Kat asked Laila if everything was OK. Laila said, "It sounds like he's talking to our landlord." A few minutes later he returned, smiling. "You won't believe this," he said. "That was the guy who owns the mall. He got a call from the Starbucks corporate office, the main one in Seattle. They're very unhappy. Can you believe that?"

285

Kat looked out the window at the line, then saw what was probably the Starbucks manager looking at them from their front door. She also saw Cooper's truck parked directly in front of the coffee shop. *Great,* she thought, *he's back at my effin' Starbucks.* She turned back to Manny. "What did you say?"

"I told him to look at the dates on our lease. I was here a year before they were, and the lease is with my corporation, we can call the shop anything we want. When he leased to Starbucks I complained, but there was nothing I could do. They assumed we would just give up and go away."

Kat looked at the crowd waiting outside the shop. "Looks like they were wrong about you going away, doesn't it?"

"Uh, guys?" said Laila, nearly overwhelmed.

"Sorry," said Kat, returning to her station, "who's next?"

"I believe I am?" said a familiar voice.

It was Cooper. Juanita had a saying that when the going got tough you should look like a duck: cool and calm on the surface while you're little webbed feet are paddling for all they're worth under the water. This was one of those moments Kat needed to be a duck. "No corporate coffee today?" she said. Snarky, but it was the best she could do.

"Thought I'd give the new guys a whirl."

"Well, I know you like to try every shop in LA, looking for… What is it you're looking for again?"

"That's a good question. How about a Caffé Americano?"

"We just call it a regular coffee," said Kat.

"Fair enough," said Cooper.

She poured his coffee and put it on the counter in front of him. "Anything else?"

"Well, I did get one of these." He showed her the door hanger Tina had given him. "This cute, but kind of angry Asian girl gave it to me."

"Just kind of?"

"She was pretty pissed."

"What was her problem?"

"It's complicated." He looked at the cookie racks. "Those peanut butter aren't made with that frozen dough, are they?"

"Sir, as you can see, there are other people waiting, so if you'd like a few more minutes to decide…"

"Sorry, they just all look so good. OK, make it a peanut butter."

"Anything else?" Kat said, dropping his cookie in a paper envelope.

"She tell you my dirty little secret?"

"Yeah. Would have been nice to hear it from you."

"Kind of hard when you don't return my calls."

"I meant before the salmon and the wine and glass slipper and candles. Especially before the candles."

"Are you ordering?" complained the guy waiting behind Cooper, 'cause I've been waiting, like, twenty minutes."

287

Cooper leaned into the counter so he could lower his voice. "You're right, Kat. I am so sorry. I'll never keep anything from you again."

"What makes you think there's going to be an again?" she said.

"'Cause I have to believe when something felt that right there has to be one."

"And why should I believe you now?"

"Because believing is what you do."

Kat was suddenly aware of how many people were crowded into her tiny space. *Could there be a worse time to have this conversation?* "It appears I'm over that," she said as she placed the sadly bagged cookie on the counter between them, next to his coffee. "You want anything else?"

"Just you," said Cooper.

"That doesn't seem to be on the menu."

He patted the counter with his palm thoughtfully.

"So, there you are," she said, indicating his cookie and coffee.

He smiled wanly. "Sorry, I think I better take a rain check," he said, and turned to leave.

"Finally," said the guy who'd been waiting semi-patiently behind him. "I need a cappuccino and two of the lemon bars."

Cooper reached the door as Tina entered. "Hi," he greeted her as they passed.

"Hi," Tina answered automatically, watching him for a moment as he crossed the lot to his truck. She looked back at Kat, who shrugged at her quizzical look. Tina muttered, "Shit," and pushed her way through to the counter, where she leaned into Kat, invading the lemon bar guy's space. "So, did he grovel?"

"Totally."

"Excuse me," said the lemon bar guy, "she's was taking my order."

"Don't make me hurt you," Tina snarled without looking at him. She leaned closer to Kat so there would be no further interruptions. "And…?"

"Now I know why I stayed with Marty so long. He couldn't break my heart because I never trusted him with it."

"OK, you might be the dumbest white girl on the planet. You walk around with these dreams of this perfect prince, but real live guys are complicated, messy and prone to stupidity. And, know what? We deal with it. Because, corny as it sounds, we complete each other."

"My mother never got over it, Teen. She's as much of a ghost as her sister."

"You're not your mother, you're Supergirl. You can leap tall buildings at a single bound, run departments at dysfunctional companies, and bake awesome peanut butter cookies the entire neighborhood is lined up to buy. You don't need the rescue—you take care of business just fine, and that means you get to have a real man, not one of the fairy tale kind, who are just frogs in satin pants anyway. I mean basically all they have going is the hair and the abs. Have you honestly ever tried to have a real conversation with one?"

Kat looked at her shop, at the busy Laila and Manny and the line of customers snaking out the door, and she smiled. "How'd you get so smart?"

"Spinach. Lots and lots of spinach. And garlic," added Tina, as Kat grabbed Cooper's coffee and cookie and headed towards the door.

"What the hell?" said the lemon bar guy.

"I can help you," said Tina, moving around the counter, suddenly the very picture of spunky politeness.

§

Cooper was backing out of the parking space when he heard a woman say "Excuse me?" He stopped, thinking he might have nearly hit someone, and Kat appeared beside the truck.

"Hi," he said, surprised.

Kat put her hand on the truck's door. "Do you know why I didn't call you back?"

"No."

"I've never hurt like that before, and I couldn't imagine any explanation that would justify what happened. I mean, if I'd at least known about her."

"You're right. Look, the best thing I can do, the only thing, is to promise to never keep anything from you again. That is, if there might be an again."

"You're divorced?"

"Yes."

"How long?"

"Little over a year, separated two years before that."

"And she's in a mental hospital."

"More like an in-patient treatment center for the wealthy insane."

"Oh, that sounds much better."

"Not to the people who run the place, they think it's a spa."

Kat thought about this, studying his face.

"Did you put her there?"

"No, her parents did."

"That's not what I meant," she said, searching his eyes.

"I knew what you meant. Look, I'll tell you anything you want to know about Sally, but it isn't really a parking lot conversation. Do you want to take a drive?"

"Got to get back to work. Big day for me."

Cooper looked at the people lined up in front of Kat's bakery. "I know, look at that. It's great. I shouldn't have come today, I mean, you have enough on your plate."

"You gonna' change the locks on your house?"

"I already did," he said, surprised again, demonstrating that even extremely smart guys not only frequently don't know when they're blowing it, they also often don't realize when they're doing pretty well. He looked into her eyes and she returned his gaze unafraid, and they both liked what they saw there.

Cooper indicated the coffee and cookie bag in her hand. "You offer curb service?"

"You have no idea," she said, leaning into the window as far as she could.

In fact, Cooper got the idea no problem, and went in for a gentle kiss. "It's not exactly a princely white steed," he said, his lips still close to hers.

"Oddly, it turns out I actually prefer old red trucks. But we still need to get that fender fixed."

"No way, that dent has serious sentimental value," he said, grazing her face with his fingertips, and she melted back into his kiss, the deepest hottest kiss two lovers had ever shared in the history of the world. . .

Made in the USA
Charleston, SC
07 March 2012